WHERE MACHINES REDEEM THE LOST

BOOKS BY BENJANUN SRIDUANGKAEW

MACHINE MANDATE

Machine's Last Testament

Then Will the Sun Rise Alabaster

And Shall Machines Surrender

Now Will Machines Hollow the Beasts

Shall Machines Divide the Earth

Where Machines Redeem the Lost

HER PITILESS COMMAND

Winterglass

Mirrorstrike

Scale-Bright

The Archer Who Shot Down Suns (collection)

WHERE MACHINES REDEEM THE LOST

BENJANUN SRIDUANGKAEW

PRIME BOOKS

WHERE MACHINES REDEEM THE LOST

Cover art by Rashed AlAkroka.

Print ISBN: 978-1-60701-548-2
Ebook ISBN: 978-1-60701-549-9

Prime Books
www.prime-books.com

For more information, contact: primer@prime-books.com

CHAPTER ONE

From the outside, the Garden of Atonement is the picture of its reputation: the prison-world of briars and knives, the labyrinth from which there is no escape. Its swarm of aegis-plates and anchor-nodes shines a pale, pulsating red. Recadat thinks of the afterlife, the layered, complex courts of hell where the dead are judged and assigned punishment tailored to their crimes. Hyper-specifically so, a bespoke experience for every sinner.

She's been allowed one sense—sight—and so she is able to watch as the outer walls, thin as knives and just as sharp, clench shut around the carrier ship that has brought her and the rest of its human cargo.

Today she will be one out of four admitted to this place. She's been dreaming of a sky bruised by dusk, though there will be no sky here. There will be nothing here, and for a year she will be nothing too.

She is hooded before being loaded into a wheelchair; her hearing is disabled, and so she has no idea whether her fellow inmates have been subjected to the same or if it is only her who has been robbed of mobility, senses, dignity—a first taste of the humiliation to come. Her implants have been ripped out long ago, and so she lacks even the gyroscopes that would let her know whether she's moving or if she is being left behind.

Eventually the hood is removed. She is strapped into the chair still. The room around her is immense, walled on all sides by mirrors. Fear comes to her at a remove—even her own limbic system does not belong to her; like everything else, it belongs to the Garden of Atonement now.

In a moment, a voice speaks, "I've just injected you with a cathartic agent. You should be regaining your hearing, but your nerves will stay anesthetized for now. You can't see or feel me—I'm working on the back of your neck, and I'm about to reinstall your network implants."

Recadat imagines the base of her skull cut open, exposed to

gleaming bone and spinal cord. A tide of blood, quickly stoppered by sealant to convenience the operation. She is cut off from pain; could even hemorrhage out and would never know until the last neuron fires and light extinguishes behind her eyes. It would be gentle.

The minutes tick by. The angle of her head makes it impossible to see who's behind her in the mirror—all she can see is her own lap and feet, the glassy ground that throws back a reflection of the smooth, non-reflective ceiling.

Her overlays come online. Information trickles: she is not connected to any network, but after this long without it is nearly a flood. Her own vitals, oxygen and hormone levels, intraocular pressure (elevated) and blood pressure (highly elevated). Data on the quality of the air she's inhaling (clean), a report on the remaining anesthesia and paralytic agents—both are diminishing in levels, being absorbed and removed by the cathartic injection. A battle of attrition within her arteries.

Sensation returns. It folds her in half: she bends and vomits, a surge of bile. The reek is sour and immediate—her olfactory nerves are working again.

"Khun Recadat Kongmanee." The voice is melodious, that midpoint between alto and tenor that could be rounded up or down in either direction. "Can you stand?"

"No." Her voice is hoarse. She continues to stare at the ground.

"Very well."

Two hands slide under her, lifting her without effort. In a moment it is no longer possible to avoid seeing her captor. Her overlays inform her they are a hundred sixty-five centimeters, about her height, yet they have no trouble carrying her. Smooth-skinned, though they would be—this must be one of the AI wardens. A face of chiseled features, with irises that rotate between daffodil yellow and the precise green of poison frogs.

"I am Ravana's Beguiling," the AI says, his accent one of thrumming music: like stringed instruments. "One of the three AIs that administer this facility."

"In the Garden of Atonement," Recadat says through a parched mouth, "I'm entitled to certain rights."

"Two to be exact. First is the right to survive: no warden will inflict fatal damage—salvation cannot be granted to the dead, that'd defeat the point of our institution. Second is the right to choose your primary warden. We're going to meet my colleagues now so you may make your decision."

He makes it sound mundane, routine, and for him it most likely is. Between her nightmares of slow strangling and her worse waking reality, Recadat studied as much as she could about this facility once she was told she'd be transferred here. That was not easy in her previous prison where no inmates were allowed network access and information was both the highest currency and the least reliable one, trading the coins of half-truths and hearsay. Two rights, one year. After that, a person walks free. Full amnesty under any jurisdiction, a sizable stipend with which to begin a new life wherever one chooses. But her life has been on loan from the start.

The corridor is empty. When she peers over Ravana's shoulder, she finds the path behind them has smoothed out, blank: no doors, no trace of the mirrored room.

He brings her into yet another room. She is placed on a low chair that makes her feel dwarfed, even more so when she sees how tall the other two AIs are—one is two meters, the other not much less. Potted ferns with razor leaves fill the corners, their tips glinting like needlepoints.

Recadat holds herself still as they look her over. To twitch a single muscle seems tantamount to losing everything: her one chance, her admission here.

The tallest of them bends until they are face to face with her. "Khun Recadat. Allow me introduce myself—I am Wisdom of Vishrava. Would you tell us your crime, that which brought you here to earn salvation?"

"That's in my profile."

"We'd like to hear it from your mouth." This from Ravana's Beguiling standing behind her, his voice even. "It's an important step in the process."

With the return of her senses comes the return of terror, though by now it is a familiar companion. The sear of it through her gut, the constriction as though her throat is filling with termites. She was fearless, once. Wildness ran through her veins like lightning. "Two years ago I attempted to destroy the core of the AI known as Chun Hyang's Glaive." And came close to it, as close as any human ever has, a near-perfect act of vengeance. "In the eye of the Mandate, it was a grave crime."

"And why did you do that?" Wisdom of Vishrava traces the line of her jaw with a long, blunt finger. "You can tell us everything."

This is not part of the script, at least not the one she rehearsed. Her pulse spikes. "Chun Hyang wronged me."

For minutes none of the AIs speak. Ventilated air currents move across the ferns and pluck them like strings: they grow louder and louder in her ears, in the way that sound itself can turn claustrophobic. Recadat tries to contain her heartbeat—knows it is fruitless—and tries not to think of anything at all, of the prospect of being ejected from here, of returning to the other facility. The prison of gradual poisons, of sudden violence.

"Now we give you a choice." The third AI turns her to em, the way a doll might be turned. Ey is statuesque, chassis and limbs done in pseudoskin—the most human-looking of them. "I am Mahiravanan's Victory, and I will take all the parts in you that are flawed and ailing, and I'll shatter those. When your year is up, you'll come out of the Garden of Atonement a new and purified being; you'll be cleansed of your need to harm, your thirst for blood and killing."

Wisdom of Vishrava tips her head up by the chin, making her look into xer face. "Here is the method by which I'll be your corrective. I will hone you and temper you, so that instead of softening or bending in this place, you will become a weapon. Sharp and terrible and beautiful, absolute in yourself. For the rest of your life, you will always have that."

Ravana's Beguiling puts his hand on Recadat's shoulder, firm. "I propose differently. I'm what you would call an eccentric among AIs, Khun Recadat, and I'm in the market for a wife. For the months you are with us, I shall jewel you and lavish you with delights; I'll see to your every need and want, and ensure your greatest comfort. Why, by the end of it you might not even want to leave."

She thinks of a hare or a fawn cornered by tigers. Disgust lances through her. Once, the woman she loved called her a tiger. She was not prey until the prison changed her. Tigers. The brightness of their coats, the glint of their eyes. She used to feel emotions other than fear.

"Do I have to choose now?" she says, once she finds her voice. All three look back at her, not responding: answer enough. And of course she knows none of it is what it seems, that there is no right choice, that all will end in terror. The only difference is in degree. The only possible strategy is to endure. She shuts her eyes, but it is impossible to ignore their hands on her, their proximity. "I'm putting myself in your care, Wisdom of Vishrava."

The other AIs withdraw their touches. Only Vishrava's remains on her cheek. When Recadat opens her eyes again, Ravana's Beguiling and Mahiravanan's Victory are gone. She never heard them leave. She is fairly certain they were physical proxies—Ravana carried her, Mahiravanan rotated her seat—but now she is less sure. Already her sense of the real slips. She swallows.

Of the three, Vishrava looks the least human: a gleaming metal figure of gold and bronze, two meters tall, long white hair that stirs about xer shoulders like living asps. The proxy's features are strong, lush mouth and elegant jawline and cheekbones. A work of calligraphy, all bold brushstrokes. Recadat has not been paying proper attention, was too preoccupied, and only now does she take in that the AI wears a dress of scarab-wing fabric. Sleek and form-fitting, the front of it split down to show full breasts and taut stomach. Leviathan plating and electrum links embellish the clothes. A vision of contrasts, stark and striking.

The AI smiles down at Recadat, an expression that seems impossible on a face built to resemble carved metal. "You should be able to move now. But I can carry you, if you prefer."

She doesn't move. "I've had tactical training."

Vishrava tucks a strand of Recadat's hair behind her ear. She tries not to flinch. "I'm aware. But first we will get you comfortable and settled. You may have misunderstood the basis of my program. In the outside world, soldiers are broken first and then they are molded into the shape of their institution's choosing. The result is brittle; their functions fail outside specific circumstances, and they can be dangerous without meaning to be. When I think of weapons, Khun Recadat, I think of instruments that last. I think of their sear and the delight of their precise edge, of how they will neither shatter under stress nor indiscriminately lash out."

Recadat makes herself untense. "I can't say that I understand."

"You expect punishment. You expect pain." The AI takes her hand, helping her to her feet. xer fingertips are surprisingly warm. "And it is true, an attempt to destroy one of us carries grave consequences, being that you're under Mandate jurisdiction. But you've suffered enough. Where you came from you had human wardens, who are steered by feelings. Here it will be different."

She breathes out as she is guided out of the room. Another corridor, this one lined in copper carpeting, the walls done in glistening red. The inside of an artery, she thinks. "Do you make these same offers to every intake?"

"Not at all. We tailor our offers to each penitent, building around their weaknesses, the scaffold of their history—their predisposition, their response range—though the core program is the same. The Garden of Atonement is rehabilitative. I was surprised you didn't choose Ravana; his is a comfortable option. Are you gender-incompatible with him and concerned it would have been unsavory? He uses personal pronouns simply to interface with humans, of course, most of us are not gendered as such."

"His proposal—it didn't work for me, that's all." Recadat throttles back memories of Chun Hyang's Glaive.

"And you are, I suspect, traumatized from what Chun Hyang did to you and would not consent to close relationship with another AI."

She is not *traumatized*. Not in that way. Chun Hyang and she met on an abattoir world, where they formed a partnership for a deadly game. The rest of it was minor details. But she keeps her mouth shut. Too early for her to show that she has opinions.

Vishrava brings her through a gate, into a solarium. Cylindrical, walled in panels of gleaming black metal, small waterfalls pouring down in silver columns. Wisterias and clematises cascade down between them, in deep purple and lavender and sudden slashes of magenta, filling the air with their perfume.

Two other inmates are here, neither of them accompanied by their warden. One is an old man who avoids her eyes. The other is a person barely out of adolescence—twenty-five at the very most, svelte and pallid, their hair kept in two thick braids. They study her with undisguised curiosity.

Vishrava leads her past this, into yet more twisting corridors and spiraling stairs, and finally into a room. "This will be your living quarters," the AI says.

White rose petals drift gently through the air, particulate light, but calibrated so well that they feel like the real thing when they touch her: velvet and gossamer. The room is large—very large, ten or twelve times the size of the cell in the detention center she spent far too long at. A bed big enough for three, a door that she hopes leads to a bathroom, a walk-in wardrobe. The walls are unadorned black glass, and it takes Recadat a full minute to realize such empty glass must serve as a canvas—either to show a view of the user's choice or to project a décor of her preferences. She hasn't been given access to such comforts for so long, comforts she once took for granted and which now seem like impossible luxuries. Even the walk-in wardrobe seems preposterous. She owns nothing at all, not even the shapeless clothes she's wearing.

"What am I supposed to do with this place?" she says quietly, standing there in the middle of what looks, now, like untold opulence.

"Sleep," Vishrava says. "Or eat. I can bring food here for you, if you'd rather not take meals in the dining room." Xe pulls furniture out of a wall: a rhomboid table with nacreous trims, two seats backed with redwood fretwork.

"This all seems expensive." A shiver goes through Recadat: not from cold—the temperature is regulated for her comfort, twenty-two degrees Celsius according to her overlays—but from her own nerves, the jangling as fear competes with a hundred thousand other factors.

Vishrava sits on one of the chairs xe's just produced, likely to minimize xer size and the threat xe represents. "We don't run cost-benefit analyses here, as it were. It does not cost so much to accommodate a person in ease. Beyond that, would you say gentleness has no effect on a person's actions? Can kindness and affection not change a human's behavior?"

Despite her determination to show no trace of personality, Recadat's mouth twists. "I don't know if that has anything to do with weapons."

"The foundation of a good weapon is sturdy material. Good alloys, structural integrity, the seamless harmony of every component. You were familiar with weapons, I believe, in your career as a public security officer."

"Is that what my profile shows, that gentleness and I get along?" A dossier of her psyche, as observed over her sentence. In that time her detention wardens delved into every corner, mapped every point of topography, or so they believed.

"In the Garden of Atonement we iterate on our philosophies, operational criteria, and pedagogy. Result is what matters, Recadat, not any satisfaction we might derive from the process. And I am not a sadist."

People can say anything. *I am not a sadist.* Her hands close. She opens them before they tighten into fists. More than anything she must maintain self-control. "Have I got a schedule?"

"We will discuss it tomorrow. For now you should get settled in—the wardrobe has clothes that will adjust to fit you, we can talk about styles when you're in the mood. You can let me know the scents you prefer for your toiletries. The ones I've prepared mostly smell like orange blossom. Inoffensive, I should think."

Should think. In truth an AI *knows*, in absolute terms, measuring against human averages. "Thank you." This comes out of her automatically—stupid. She's resolved to show compliance, but not to show her belly like a beaten dog, to let herself turn dissolute and undone. There was enough of that in the prison.

Vishrava inclines xer head. "May I touch you?"

All of her wants to say no. But she must endure. "Yes."

The AI cradles the side of Recadat's face, and painfully she thrills to it: the sheer skin starvation, those years incarcerated with the occasional stint in isolation. The Wisdom of Vishrava should be icy, xer chassis shell frictionless, but instead xer hand is warm. It is everything Recadat wants.

Vishrava runs xer thumb over Recadat's mouth. Then xe lets go. "I will see you soon."

CHAPTER TWO

The next morning she jolts to consciousness as though electrocuted by the force of her own volition—as if all her neurotransmitters fired at once, in a concerted effort to break her dreams like so much spun salt. Recadat remembers the dreams because the humiliation follows even into her waking moments. They're never cohesive recreations of true memory but for hours after she will feel hounded, stalked by the shadow of a tall broad-shouldered woman, a ghost of hard bulk and wolfish appetite. In some of the dreams she's devoured whole. In others she's pinned down and parted and then annihilated.

When she pulls herself free of the sheets, she half-expects them to transform into snakes, into grasping hands tipped in talons.

But they are just sheets, and when she tries the door she finds that it opens easily. For a moment she focuses on her own respiratory functions, the open and close of it, the rhythm of bronchial whispers. She doesn't attempt to leave: just because the door is unlocked does not mean she has freedom. Sometimes it means the opposite. The human wardens played such games.

Now comes the time to orient herself. She measures the dimensions of her room, makes sure that there's only one apparent point of entry—though even that can be fluid—and then she gets clean. She doesn't relax into or enjoy the hot shower, the soaps and creams that smell—as Vishrava promised—like orange blossom. All of it can be taken away at any time. The only path is to hold nothing dear, and therefore to possess nothing that can be lost. It is easy. She has had practice.

She wonders if Vishrava has ever seen real orange blossoms. Likely yes. Recadat imagines what the AI used to be. All three wardens' names follow a motif but that is hardly informative, may well have been what they took up after they assumed control of the Garden of Atonement, as a private joke. There is history: this place used to belong to a religious order, a minor ascetic sect whose priests handed out bloody penitence. Absolution could be found in the rawness of bruises and lacerations, in the smell of lymph and the crack of the whip. She walked into this place expecting to see it a charnel house.

The provided wardrobe makes her think of bhikkhunis: so much white. But it is more decadent than it first looks, the fabrics underlaid with roseate and moonstone hues. There are pleated blouses so angular they look sculpted, voluminous skirts that move like seafoam. Both are too feminine for her, but she finds a fitted shirt, a suit jacket and the trousers to match. They settle onto her as though they've been tailor-made, and faint calligraphic lines bud across the material as they adjust to her frame. She feels a little more like herself.

She is hungry, but she's learned to tolerate it well. In a little shelf facing her bed she finds rose-tinted bottles. Plain water, cold and clear. From the bottle's frigid mouth she sips, little by little. Access to the room's controls has been granted to her, temperature regulation, lighting and particulate ornamentation. She touches none of them.

When Vishrava enters the room, it is with a covered tray that xe carries adroitly, despite its generous size. Xe puts it on the dining table and xer mouth quirks, wry. "I see you haven't taken advantage of our entertainment options. Or even decorated this room. Do you prefer minimalism?"

"I didn't know there were entertainment options."

The AI uncovers the tray: jasmine rice, basil pork stir-fry, a bowl of green curry. All food particular to the cuisine of Recadat's homeworld. "We have media libraries you can download. Not the latest, and we don't produce our own, but there's a large range—serialized shows, films with options for virtuality participation and without, texts of all kinds, music, games. Even erotic content, if that strikes your fancy."

Nothing could strike her fancy any less. "Sure. I'll take a look."

"It'll keep you from getting too bored. A well-stimulated mind goes a long way. But first let's see to you getting fed."

When Recadat eats, she does so at a measured pace. To show eagerness or enjoyment, or even to admit to hunger, means that her next meal might be delayed or her current one might be knocked or snatched out of her hands. That was the case at her previous prison, and she has no reason to expect any different here. Still it is good—overwhelming her palate, the distinct taste of fish sauce, the spice in the stir-fry, even the jasmine fragrance of the rice. She has to exert the most discipline she's ever needed in months to keep her expression indifferent.

"This was cooked by one of my other charges," Vishrava says, pouring a cup of lemongrass tea. Xer albino hair is inert today. "You don't have to work, naturally—Mahiravanan, Ravana and I can do anything that requires delicacy and we automate the rest with drones. But some people enjoy keeping busy, or enjoy cooking as a pastime. I had to look around for someone who's familiar with your cuisine. Is this to your liking?"

"It's flavorful." In fact it is excellent. "You have another Ayothayan here?" For a split second she wonders if it is *her*, the woman who haunts Recadat's dream. That obsession. But of course it couldn't possibly be.

"No, my charge is from Krungthep Station. Similar cultural and demographic makeup. Do you want to talk about Ayothaya?"

"I haven't been back there since it was liberated." Too fraught a place. Too fraught—everything. Her fingers twitch. She forces them to still.

"Ayothaya's saviors were unusual," xe goes on. "A human and an AI, though their identities have been obfuscated—it wouldn't do for a Mandate member to interfere so dramatically and publicly. What do you think?"

"I have no opinion."

Vishrava looks at her but does not press. "I should introduce you to your new home, and to your cohabitants."

Cohabitants—what a toothless word, a select euphemism, as though she and the others have come here of their own free will: a meditative retreat under the benevolent guidance of three AIs who have styled themselves after demons. All the same she smiles and falls into step, lets Vishrava put a hand on the small of her back. Such a careful gesture it is, chivalrous, yet a reminder whose control she is under. She let herself fall apart during her intake; it is not an error she intends to repeat.

In a lounge, two inmates—alerted to and likely pre-informed about her—are waiting. One mid-board game in the corner. The other is at the piano, an instrument of copper wood and brilliant teeth. All conversation and music cease on Vishrava's arrival.

"This is Recadat." Vishrava presents her the way xe might present a prize student or a piece of art freshly made, proudly tempered. "She will join us from today onward."

The pianist straightens from her seat, giving Recadat an once-over. She is a woman in deep, lustrous red, a dress of tight bodice and skirts that look as though they are made from panes of warped glass. Recadat immediately tenses—too much like Chun Hyang's Glaive. The woman notices. "Well, hello there," she drawls. "I'm Ceres. You're very pleasant on the eye. What is your background?"

"Public security," Recadat says.

This makes the boardgame player straighten. "Now we don't get one of those every day." Ey tips eir head at her; faint cobalt glints in the black prairie of eir hair. "I'm Zerjic. Welcome to our odd little club. We're all in Vishrava's care here, and bless xer for xer patience with us."

"You all make it so easy." The AI bends down to kiss Zerjic on the mouth, light, quick. She does the same with Ceres. "I'll leave you here to acclimate to one another. How do you all feel about a shared dinner tonight?"

The two murmur their assent. Recadat makes noise to the same effect. It is just as well—she needs to assess them, threat and risk factors, whether they will be enemies or allies. A simple binary, and through it she can get her bearings. Ever since the prison, that has always been the easiest way for her to understand the world: friend or foe, safety or danger.

Vishrava leaves. For a time they regard each other in silence. Recadat looks for marks of visible trauma on Ceres and Zerjic—fresh injuries, scarring, any sign of lacerations or broken bones. None seem in evidence. Ceres is full-figured, soft-looking, not someone Recadat would read as a threat in the wild. Zerjic is her opposite: thick biceps and thick thighs under eir trousers and eigenvector shirt, powerful shoulders, a jawline that could slice glass.

"So." Zerjic gestures at the chair across eir board. "Before we came here, all of us were in Mandate detainment for heinous sins. What's yours? I'm asking sincerely. Vishrava didn't show us your dossier or anything, that'd be a violation of privacy."

Privacy in a place like this is mere illusion, Recadat might say, but there's no gain in belaboring the obvious. "Tell me yours," she says. "I'm at a disadvantage."

Ceres and Zerjic exchange looks, speculative. Perhaps they have made bets, a pool of two guessing at her sins. Developing theories based on how she looks, how she carries herself. They would both be wrong.

"I'm in here for a heist." Ceres lifts her hands from the piano, clipping on a set of nail guards long enough to be claws: they are elaborately made, a silver base embellished by jagged crystal motifs, gold and garnet and tourmaline. "That is to say, I stole a sacred ship from the Vatican. They got me five years after the fact—really hold a grudge. What with this treaty and that, the Mandate paid for my transfer from a Vatican detention facility. They were curious how such a place affected my psychological profile, whether I was successfully converted to Catholicism. I wasn't, by the way. They *tried* though, wanted to make me a nun and everything—hilarious."

Petty theft, Recadat thinks. Mundane. In her previous profession she would not have spent more than a minute assessing Ceres; no point building a criminal profile. "And you?"

Zerjic makes a little gesture. "I got involved with a scheme to help a Mahakala heiress get into Shenzhen Sphere, not completely legally."

As far as she knows, Shenzhen takes their immigration control with brutal seriousness. "Did you have a death wish?"

Eir laugh is slow and smooth, decadent. "I had a lot of ambition; the heiress was going to pay well. Go on—tell us yours."

Recadat puts herself on a chaise lounge not far from the piano. The furniture, like Ceres' dress, is themed after crystals and glass, complex silicate structures. The armrest has the appearance of bismuths lashed together haphazardly. "I tried to destroy an AI's core."

Zerjic whistles. "And you asked if *I* had a death wish. How close did you get?"

"Enough that the AI felt threatened." She folds her hands in her lap. "I'm not trying to brag." Vishrava and the rest would be watching, in any case. What she does not admit is that at the time she *did* have a death wish.

"Oh, but it *is* worth bragging about." Ceres leans forward. "You're going to tell us how you managed the feat."

"I don't think so." Not that the help she received is the kind she will disclose or betray. They swore her to secrecy, and she's dutifully kept to it even under torture.

"Pay no attention to Ceres. She likes to be seditious." Zerjic grins abruptly. "How long are you staying here? I have eight months to go. Ceres has seven, but she doesn't behave so it keeps getting extended."

"A year." Recadat winces at this reflexive openness: when did she begin to answer questions so easily and mindlessly. A habit built as a defense—when she has something to hide, she loosens all else, a deluge of answers that don't matter to bury and conceal the secret. "What is Vishrava like?"

"Lenient," says Zerjic.

"Attractive," offers Ceres. "Xe's one of those AIs who will have sex with humans."

Recadat doesn't ask how Ceres knows that; resolves to specifically never ask about that. For a second time she looks over the other inmates. Zerjic has a full mouth and a deep umber complexion: Sinhalese she thinks, from Vishnu's Leviathan or Sinhapura perhaps, though ey would blend into dozens of polities. The name is almost certainly an alias. Ceres is Korean or Chinese and keeps her hair black, threaded through with metallic strands in red and electrum. A blunt nose and full cheeks, skin in pale gold, brilliant eyes—one natural, the other gilded with a complicated ocular lens, patterned in slow-revolving stars.

Zerjic takes it upon emself to show Recadat the premises; Ceres returns to her piano. The lounge is one of their three common areas where they will eat if they're not joining the greater dining hall shared by all inmates. "Which we don't very often," ey admits as ey brings her to the gym. "This place we share with Ravana's . . . brides. They don't talk much. Quite intense. We leave them alone."

At the moment the gym is empty, one section filled with weights, running equipment, and punching bags. The other half is a hexagonal pool that smells like the sea, and a floor-to-ceiling panorama that shows a sunlit expanse, waves foaming and lapping at a distant shore. A horizon without an end. Recadat catches herself staring. It is not real—of course it is not, they are inside a hollow artificial moon—but even in image she hasn't seen anything like this for so long. No overlays. No virtuality. She tries not to count backward, measure out the time in prison. To think about it is to confront what was done to her there, the depth to which she lowered herself so she could survive—and could, eventually, reach this place.

The next spot Zerjic shows her is a second, massive solarium. Walkways crisscross the air, linking platforms cantilevered to baobab trunks and half-veiled by cascades of wisterias. Waterfalls murmur and splash; shadows of birds flit across. Recadat looks up into the vaulted ceiling of fractal glass fringed by black metal lace and green-gold leaves.

"Why is it like this?" she asks, her voice muted.

"Not as spartan as you expected?" Ey taps a low-trailing wisteria. "By some standards this is unbearable poverty, but you and I are of diminished circumstances and we must endure the best we can. In any case it's best to think of ourselves as chosen. We've already done our penance in unlovely places, why shouldn't we enjoy a comfortable halfway-house before we're out? All we need to do is behave."

But what does that mean, Recadat thinks, what does it entail. There is no freedom without a price. Even basic ease—food, shelter—must be paid for, in currency or in blood. The apparent luxury cannot be all it seems. "What is Vishrava really like?"

"You don't trust me and you don't trust xer." Ey chuckles. "That's natural. When xe says that xe'll make you a weapon, xe means that xe will make you whole. A weapon in mind and body. There'll be physical regimens, of course, but you already have the background for that—am I right? It's about regaining control over your thoughts, your nervous system, your limbic assets. It's about emerging into the outside world again ready to face whatever you've left behind."

Her chest tightens. "You sound like a therapist." Or an indoctrinated believer.

"No such thing." Zerjic holds up eir hands. "I'm an ex-convict. More so than the usual—I've been through . . . various forms of prison, let's just say. You and I are natural enemies."

"I haven't been in public security for a long time." When once that career meant everything to her. But outside Ayothaya it means nothing, and she hasn't been back on her homeworld for years. All she had left, after leaving Septet, was the vast desire to see Chun Hyang turned to cinders. And she worked toward that, careful machinations and schemes; she accepted forbidden help; she did everything perfectly.

Perfect did not suffice.

"Suppose you'd tell me why you quit being a cop?"

Recadat's facial muscles twitch. She smooths her fingers down her lapels. "Why all the quizzing?"

"We'll be sharing living space for many months."

"You said you had a Mahakala client." The planet's name tugs at her, an ache under the skin. She doesn't have the faintest idea why: it is a place to which she has no connection. "Care to tell me more?"

"It was a routine job, nothing very interesting other than the heiress being outlandishly rich. Actually, speaking of cops—let me try something."

Zerjic moves abruptly, shoving her up against a baobab trunk. She responds without thinking: stepping hard on eir foot, driving her elbow into eir solar plexus. Ey makes a noise and staggers back, narrowly avoiding the kick she aims at eir knees.

She holds herself still, breathing hard, more adrenaline than exertion. Her nerves sing. She wants to shatter bones; she wants to see the coils and wet excess of guts. But that brief contact has told her that Zerjic could have done more if ey meant to do damage. This was a test, a provocation. "What do you fucking want?"

Ey holds eir hands up, keeping eir distance. "I'm more curiosity than sense. And I wanted to see how someone who nearly killed an AI would react. If it is any consolation, I'm going to bruise *and* Vishrava is going to nail my hide to the wall."

A prospect that does not seem to disturb Zerjic too much; again she wonders what constitutes disciplinary action here, from the wardens in general or Vishrava in particular. Lenient, Zerjic said. "Don't do it again." Her palm itches. She wishes she had a small knife on her. The brandished edge is always better than the promise of a fist, even if she can do damage with both just the same. But she's suffered muscle atrophy in prison, and her augmentations are gone.

"I promise," ey says. "I may not act it, but what you did hurt. Thought you'd gouge my eyes out."

"What would the wardens have done?"

"Prevented anything fatal." Zerjic shrugs. "I also thought it'd help demonstrate to you a little that Vishrava gives us a lot of freedom."

To injure and test one another. Another layer to the AI's little games. Recadat measures her breathing and instead catches a scent of Zerjic: faint spice and something more basal. Not sweat precisely, peculiarly appealing. "I'd like to be alone for a while. Explore the place."

"Sure. You should have everything you need in your overlays to navigate the area." A pause. "Including where *not* to go."

To obey, to follow instructions precisely, to adhere to the rules both in spirit and letter. That did not keep her safe in the prison, but then her wardens there were not inclined to mercy. Chun Hyang's Glaive was one of the prison's patrons, and the AI left instructions for her sentence. She learned the precise significance, the exact definition, of what it means to experience a fate worse than death.

She remembers begging. For food, for water, for a cessation of pain; for clothing when it became too cold. She remembers screaming until her voice broke as they put her eye out, and then the wet noises of her mucus and tears and parched sobbing. The stink of her own piss and voided bowels. The eye was restored since—part of the doctrine of humane correction, the same as the Garden of Atonement's, that a prisoner must remain whole in body. Not always the mind, but that is a component that reconstruction cradles and implants can't heal and so it was never part of the requisites. Over and over she was carved open and unmade, and over and over they put her back together. All for the sin of attempting an AI's true destruction, one of the gravest crimes as the Mandate accounts such things.

Panic scrabbles behind her ribs. She inhales and tries to slow it down. The first time she saw her body, naked in more ways than one after the forced excisions, she was nauseated: the gauntness, the thrust of her pelvic bones that seemed ready to pierce what little flesh she had left. And the scars, the innumerable scars, where her implants had been.

She climbs a long metal bridge. Railings extend as she steps on, high enough that she would have to make a concerted effort to climb them, at which point she doesn't doubt one of the wardens will dispatch their proxies to bring her to safety. Or else there are drones hidden in the alcoves or tangles of liana vines, ready to prevent suicide attempts.

No one else is here. Recadat wonders how many inmates are in the Garden of Atonement. She is familiar with the logistics of holding facilities from the jailer's end; it was unavoidable in public security. Three prisoners were brought here with her and though she never made their acquaintance—they were surveilled and isolated on that ship—she would be able to recognize their faces, based on a few brief glimpses. She has not yet seen them. She may spend her entire year without ever seeing those three. If they are still alive. *First is the right to survive*, Ravana said, but she does not trust even that. The time when machines could not lie was long past.

The ascent stabilizes her. In the prison there was no gym, barely any space to stretch her legs. Now she can walk, refamiliarize herself with the small alchemies of the sartorius muscle, the minor miracles that enable motor functions. Things she took for granted and which, she later learned, should have been treasured and cherished all along.

The air here is so clean. Recycled, it would have to be, but filtered so well that it doesn't smell stale. She runs her fingers along the railing but finds she can leave no marks—oleophobic glass. Likely difficult to break as well. Her overlays are no longer connected to sensors that'd let her view and analyze the material composition of a wall, a piece of furniture; her perception is now one of guesswork, trial-and-error, where she used to understand the world with a machine's intuition and accuracy. Now her overlays inform her no further than what's in front of her nose, conveying only data that the Garden of Atonement allots her: oxygen levels, her position in the permitted areas of the facility, how to reach her warden Vishrava.

Her hand curls and uncurls compulsively. She appreciates that she has fine control again, thumbs and forefinger and index finger operational once more. She pinches a wisteria, twists it off, and crumples the dew-glazed petals in her palm. Up and up she goes, her respiration running ragged as she finds her limits, but she pushes on. Little by little she shall regain her strength.

When she reaches the highest platform, she nearly collapses. Sweat streaks down her spine, gathers under her breasts and the backs of her knees. She wipes at her face and inhales deeply the fragrance of flowers and her own salt. It is no accomplishment at all, in the grand schemes of things. But it is victory of a sort, and she will take that where she finds it.

From the platform she watches the water, the soft air currents that move through the wisterias and clematises. She doesn't think of anything: there is purity in this, in physical exhaustion so thorough it leaves the mind blank. It is a good vantage point. She can observe without being seen, if any inmate enters or passes by.

Footsteps from the ramp opposite her. Odd. If someone is there, she should have seen them while she climbed. Recadat straightens and peers through the translucent railing, but the railing on the other end is frosted and even higher than hers: what she can see is a dark-skinned, bulky figure in black. Too short to be any of the wardens, too tall to be Zerjic. The figure is still, scrutinizing her back, though from their side they can't possibly discern much of her either.

A spark of recognition. She goes cold. Then she starts moving down the ramp, which obliges by extending across the baobab's parameter, budding into a bridge as she runs. Not fast enough. By the time she reaches the other side, she is doubled over with exertion, nearly gagging. The person is gone. There are only fallen clematises on the ground, crushed flat: as tender as bruised skin.

Dinner is quiet; Recadat eats to be filled, this time, to ensure she will not be hungry even if she's denied her next meal. Zerjic looks amused. Ceres looks disdainful at her table manners. Vishrava is absent, physically at least. They all know the wardens may surveil them at any and all times.

She finishes her portion of spring rolls and wipes her fingers on a serviette. "What are we supposed to do after dinner?" Before food she meant to ask Zerjic about the figure she saw in the solarium, but to inquire that much is dangerous. She can admit to nothing.

"Not much." Ey pushes eir plate of spring rolls toward her, the same way ey might with a child or a pet ey wishes to spoil. An apology for what ey did in the solarium, perhaps. "This is your first day, so make the best of it. Tomorrow there will be prayers and instructions in moral clarity, classes that'll get you technical certifications or academic skills if you need any for when you venture out in the universe. Gym sessions. Nothing strenuous. This is a healing place."

"This is a healing place," Ceres echoes, mocking. "Zerjic is such an obedient little convert. You and I know better, don't you, Recadat?"

Recadat takes the spring rolls, savoring the scent of sesame oil and seasoned chicken. "I don't know what you mean."

"Ey may brag about eir checkered past, but ey is domesticated." Ceres lifts her glass of wine and smiles over its rim. "I've been here longer. There are things I want to find out about the Garden of Atonement, and there are things I know Zerjic doesn't. You strike me as someone who's cognizant that all of this has a price, that the AIs aren't doing this out of charity or even in pursuit of some lofty moral goals—AIs don't *have* morals. What profit are they getting out of it? Are we the goods and if so what currency are we being traded for, and how?"

Zerjic gestures with eir blunt, elegant hand. "Ceres has a lot of conspiracy theories. That is one of her favorites. Incidentally the real reason Ceres has been here for close to two years now is because she has a fetish for AIs, and this is where she can be closest to them short of applying for tourist visas to Shenzhen Sphere."

"Discernment is not a fetish, Zerjic, unless one is a fool." The woman scoffs. "Two years are the hard limit, anyway, so I'll be out of here soon enough. But in the meantime I'll wring out all its secrets. I was Ravana's when I first came here, but Vishrava took over my care."

"What did he offer you?" And what did Vishrava, for that matter.

"Wouldn't you like to know?" Ceres drains her glass of claret. "I'll make you a deal. I can tell you everything I know about the Garden of Atonement. In exchange, when you get around to it—and I suspect that's what xe picked you for—give me a record of what fucking Vishrava is like, a virtuality capture is best but footage will do. I'm academically interested."

Recadat does not bother to look shocked; Zerjic has provoked her in one way, and Ceres has chosen another. "I have no intention of doing any such thing."

To that Ceres merely laughs.

Curfew begins an hour after dinner—too short a period to explore the area or return to the solarium. She returns to her room: easy enough to pretend at docility for the time being.

Once she's locked the door behind her, she strips and passes her hands over her sternum, down her abdomen where her skeleton presses against the thin sheath of skin, where she can feel individual vertebrochondral ribs like brittle wood. The anatomy of diminishment. One year. She may be able to regain some muscle and stamina. Neither will avail her against the wardens, but she wants to hold her own against other inmates: Zerjic has shown her she will require that. What's been taken from her she will never have again, yet that doesn't mean she needs to accept being a husk.

Vishrava promised media libraries. Recadat browses them,

desultory, too restless to sleep yet. She finds a vast catalogue, media visual or textual in every category she's heard of and several she hasn't. Fiction and nonfiction. Brainless dramas, stark plays in monochrome, treatises on political systems. She can indulge herself the entire year in a single medium without repeating material.

She samples the dramas—office comedies grant a glimpse into a world exotic to her, if tedious and absurdist. Fantastical time-traveling adventures show her the prehistoric past, the time before spacefaring and terraforming. Several speculative documentaries on humanity's origination planet, the great cradle whose name and location have been lost to time. Little by little she unwinds into the entertainments. An episode of the time-traveling adventure comes up where the protagonist is captured by an enemy agent, sedated and brought to a maximum-security prison. Her throat closes. This is nothing like what happened to her but all the same—the spectacle of a person lolling in restraints—hits too close to home. She shuts down the show.

Her gorge rises. Barely she reaches the bathroom in time to regurgitate everything she's just eaten. The hot surge of digested food and acid, the contraction of what feels like her entire chest cavity, the collapse of what feels like her entire digestive system. She vomits and spits and hacks. Tears burn down her cheeks as she pants and folds onto the cold marble floor.

Her eyes squeeze shut. The alabaster and silver of the bathroom are suddenly too bright. The air reeks, though the sink is already cleaning itself, sucking and wiping away the filth of her body. Soon the ventilation will erase even the stench. She almost wishes it wouldn't. Let the evidence of gross mortality remain.

A notification lets her know someone is at her door—Vishrava. She cleans her mouth and face as best she can before admitting the AI.

Vishrava looks more serpentine than when she last saw the warden, platinum scales winding up xer arms and ankles like dermal jewelry. A smattering along xer collarbones, in curlicues. Xe gives pause when xe sees her and then says, gently, "It's sixteen degrees in here and you aren't wearing anything."

Recadat stares back. "So I am not." She tries to make it sound intentional, not a result of her rushing out of the bathroom, too mindless and stricken to remember her nudity. Nor does she try to cover herself now.

"It may be wise for you to put something on." Vishrava strides past her, fetches a long loose kurta, and holds it out. "If the wardrobe isn't to your liking, you only need to tell me. Without acquiring pneumonia, for preference."

"I can't get pneumonia at sixteen degrees." She puts the kurta on, perfunctory. The fabric is clean, redolent with orange blossom, and settles on her skin like clouds.

"I was being hyperbolic. Nevertheless you're likely to get sick." Vishrava cocks her head. "I won't pretend I'm here by coincidence—I noticed you were in distress. And Zerjic will be disciplined."

No attempt at denying that prisoners are under constant surveillance. "I'll be—" Fine. No. She will not be. "I'm not always like this. I was not like this." There was barely anything in the entertainment episode, no graphic demonstration: her time in prison should not rise in her like a tide of bile.

"I would have blocked any content I thought might have disturbed you, but I suspect you wouldn't appreciate being coddled." Vishrava sits on the bed, light undulating along xer scales in odd, warped patterns. A match for the white ophidian strands of xer hair. "I'm certified to give treatment in several formats—counseling, exposure therapy, long-term welfare improvement."

"I didn't realize AIs could get certified in those." Recadat tugs at the kurta, pulling the sleeves down unnecessarily. She resists the urge to wrap her arms around herself. "Why would you bother?"

"Chun Hyang must have given you the impression that most machines regard humans with contempt and cruelty." More softly xe adds, "I am not Chun Hyang's Glaive."

She does not want to talk about Chun Hyang; she does not want to think about it, save to fantasize about its core blistering and charring to cinders. She was so close. She could have touched the warm shell of it. "If I don't improve to your satisfaction within the year, what's going to happen?"

"By then, if you want to leave you will be able to, no strings attached. If you wish to stay another year, that'll be fine too. Your choice will be respected." Vishrava pats the mattress. "I don't think I will convince you tonight of my intentions, but in practical terms I'd rather you get some sleep than I win the argument."

Recadat unclenches her hands. Spite will guide her, she decides, stronger than resolve or any of the virtues preached by the monks at home. "Fine. I'll get in bed."

"I don't believe you will be able to rest without sedatives, after everything. I've had experience providing sleep therapy. Having something warm and solid can help." The AI holds out xer hand. "Why not try it? Should I fail to be of use, I'll leave after ten minutes."

She stares at the proxy, at the physical presence of it: the rounded golden shoulders mantled in serpent-seeming, the waspish waist and high breasts. Nothing about xer looks clinical. "If you insist."

"I insist. I won't touch you any more than a hospital cradle would."

Hospital cradles are not shaped like this, Recadat could say, and Vishrava must have a proxy lying around that looks less human. Or xe could simply summon a comparable drone. But she is worn out, knows how threadbare she has become, and Vishrava is right that she needs the sleep. In the prison she got so little of it, deprivation being the point, to keep her weak and hollowed-out and witless. Sleep is a treasure, a prized resource, and she doesn't intend to be precious about it. She climbs into the bed and turns her back to Vishrava, keeping a good distance between them.

She fantasizes, as she sometimes did when she had the luxury of a bed (though in the prison none was ever this wide, this comfortable), about her life from before. Ayothaya prior to the invasion, her work in public security—work that was just and which she believed in, a partner she could trust at her back and for whom she nursed a secret infatuation. Harmless, at that point. Then came the graveyard world and the Mandate's game in which she competed to obtain her heart's desire—and lost.

Every ligament in her turns rigid when Vishrava's arm falls on her waist. "You said you weren't going to touch me."

"Not any more than a hospital cradle. I'm going to move a little closer to you. Is that all right?"

Recadat nearly says no. Defiance pushes her to say, "Yes." Because why should she be afraid of this—why should she be so abject, so despicable to herself. Chun Hyang was years ago and she will not fall into an AI's thrall again, be manipulated into that cocktail of lust and terror. Instead she must separate her cowering animal part from the rest of her, and show it no pity.

Vishrava pulls her close, tucking her against those soft breasts, that soft waist. They are astonishingly lifelike; she wonders why the AI bothers to have them rather than keeping xer proxy featureless, a map of minimalism. It is what she would have done—to be a creature that admits no vulnerability, to be anonymous and numinous. An instrument of pure will and might.

The thought lulls her to sleep, though by the time she wakes Vishrava is gone, xer side of the bed as smooth and uncreased as though Recadat slept alone the entire night.

CHAPTER THREE

Morning prayers. Recadat does not know quite what to expect as she follows Zerjic and Ceres, joining a double-file of inmates streaming toward the Hall of Peace and Cultivation. The name does not inspire optimism, though she does get the chance to see more of the Garden's population—attendance at morning orisons is mandatory. She loses count, but by her estimate there must be about a hundred twenty prisoners, give or take a dozen. She does not spot the person she's looking for and she wonders if it was a hallucination after all, a product of nerves and anxiety and wounds, as much wishful wanting as terror.

There is no uniform: she is surprised again. All prisons require one, shapeless and hideous, a crucial step in the process of dehumanization. In the Garden everyone dresses as though they are allocated a wardrobe of their own, from plain to sumptuous. Here an haute couture hanfu in ombre shades, red to purple to bruise-black, the wearer wreathed in a haze of particulate phoenixes. There a jacket assembled from prismatic panes and matte-black steel, paired with eigenvector slacks. Some wear more ordinary apparel, but even among the most austere everything is exactly tailored, flattering. The human shape is not made wretched and contemptible here. Some of the inmates even wear hairpins and toothed broaches that could be used as weapons, things that would never have been permitted in a corrective facility.

The Hall of Peace and Cultivation is an auditorium, the seats arranged in irregular rows, shaped like dark lotuses. When she drops into hers, Recadat half-expects it to fold up and trap her there, but it remains just a chair. No AI proxies are in sight, and she doesn't spot any drones. Compliance does not need to be enforced with physical force or even physical presence.

On the stage, a column has risen, an industrial stalagmite of jagged edges and faceted sheen. The hall goes silent.

It seems a trick of vision. One moment there is a dark column striated with gray; the next it has warped and flowed into the shape of Mahiravanan's Victory, a proxy twelve meters tall, folded in the padmasana position. A bodhisattva's stance. Eir eyes open, golden and enormous, and eir gaze sweeps across the hall. It transfixes—even Recadat feels pinned in place by it, a butterfly on a corkboard.

"This is a day of peace," Mahiravanan says.

The inmates intone, "And we stand to receive cleansing."

"The morning that begins in grace leads to an evening that ends in joy."

"And so we gather the days of glass to make a mirror in which our hearts may be seen, remade, purified . . . "

The call-and-response goes on, an insistent drone. She does not join in. *The bird, once freed, will never forget its cage—and thus the wild heart is tamed by chains of gold. The human soul is vast but can be folded like paper—and so our hearts will be made small in this place, this place, this place.*

By the time the prayer is over her nerves are on edge, her skin prickling with unease. The expressions of everyone around her are smooth with rapture, ecstatic. Mahiravanan's gigantic eyes fall on her as she exits the auditorium with the others, but ey does not summon or stop her. Out in the corridor, wardens appear to pick up their charges: ten proxies of Ravana's Beguiling, twelve of Mahiravanan's Victory, and seven of Vishrava. Inmates are separated into small groups and led away, presumably to their classes or correctional sessions.

A Vishrava proxy weaves through the crowd, taking her hand as it reaches her. "I have something a little different in mind," Vishrava says, guiding her away from the rest of the throng. "Ravana wanted me to bring you to a class on current events, but that doesn't seem aligned with your present interests."

"There's a . . . current events class."

"Yes, we're not keeping you cloistered and ignorant, and some of our charges have been locked up for years. By the time you leave you will be ready to rejoin society. We'll give you a synopsis of any polity you choose to travel to, and if necessary we'll provide you with the documentation and references for immigration if your destination is a place where you don't have existing citizenship. Naturally nothing can be *guaranteed* but we'll try our utmost. Shenzhen Sphere is popular, of course, and for that there's less paperwork to deal with."

Vishrava's idea of education turns out to be the gym. The AI has cleared out part of it, leaving a large rectangle softened by an equally large exercise mat. Xe hands Recadat a body sheath and makes a show of turning away while she changes.

The sheath is supple, cool against her skin: not uncomfortably so. It covers her arms, forms gloves over her hands. Her overlays let her know it has thermoregulation and impact-dispersion components. Hardly casual gym attire; more fitting for field use.

Vishrava has taken position at the center of the mat, stance relaxed. Xe beckons to Recadat. "Come at me."

"What?"

"Treat this like sparring," says the AI. "The gloves will protect your hands. If you do break something, I have other proxies."

She doesn't move. "I don't think so."

"I don't damage easily. This proxy is rated for security duties." Vishrava gestures at xer full chest, xer scaled limbs. "This isn't a test, Recadat. I'm not going to bait you into hitting me and then punish you for scratching my chassis. I'm asking for us to spar because you'll feel better, more in control. If you'd rather not, that's fine as well. I'll take you to any of the classes you'd like. Cooking, current events, team sports."

"What *do* you believe I'm capable of?"

"I read your profile," the warden says patiently. "Your marksmanship was fair, but you were at your best in hand-to-hand. In getting up close and delivering sudden, killing force. We can start there. No need to hold back. I'll defend only. We stop when you want to stop."

It is a challenge, but in her current state she's cognizant of how little she can do. Her body does not forget—muscle memory, her instructors liked to tell her, is forever—but it has lost most of its tools, has turned from honed weapon to a shriveled, beaten animal. By luck alone was she able to do what she did to Zerjic. Once her flesh was like armor; now it is less than paper, unable to shield her from the intrusions and indignations that the universe threatens. But she goes through her warm-up routines, testing her strength, stretching until her limbs grow light and her senses turn sharp.

Her respiratory tempo is even, entirely under control, when she steps onto the mat. Toppling or damaging Vishrava in any substantial way is an unrealistic goal, but she can make the attempt. Her former field partner, the woman who will not leave her dreams alone, said she had the soul of a tiger. Ferocious in battle, an appetite for violence that bordered on lust. Recadat denied it but was secretly pleased at the comparison. It meant something, to be praised in that way.

Slight as she is, she's used to fighting those bigger and broader. Vishrava moves at a speed plausible for a human beginner, then at a speed more suited to an intermediate practitioner when she blocks Recadat's jabs and experimental kicks. She stays out of the AI's range, though she knows in a real-world situation she'd be vulnerable to Vishrava's long limbs, xer massive reach—all those two meters of height, all those powerful limbs and wide hands. The impact from Vishrava's fists. Even if xe were human, it'd pack bone-shattering force.

A memory comes, unbidden, of her cartilage crunching as a prison guard's fist met her nose. The act was without rhythm or reason—they did not need to interrogate her; the facts of her crime were bare and blatant. The guard's single motivation was simple cruelty, retaliation for what she'd attempted to do to Chun Hyang. To the Mandate's human citizens, machines are holy and Chun Hyang's brush with mortality—that it was possible at all—was sacrilege.

She throttles back the flash of recall. Vishrava has barely moved from xer starting position, feet firm, no tension in shoulders or spine. Gathering herself, she darts in again, to get inside Vishrava's guard. The AI is not aggressive but is not making it easy for her to find openings.

A straightforward approach, then. She doesn't feint—simply she rushes in, within striking distance. In a real fight she would be at a severe advantage, would likely have had to sacrifice an arm to an enemy blow. Vishrava is more of a glorified training dummy. She aims low: Vishrava fends one strike off, but does not quite block the roundhouse kick that slams squarely into a knee. In a human it might have dislocated the femur and cracked the patella. Vishrava merely folds, toppling backward, but not before seizing her wrist.

Recadat falls on top of Vishrava, panting. The proxy is not damaged, that much is evident. Xe is smiling faintly.

"How are you feeling?"

"Better," she admits. "You let me win, though. Too easily."

"Once you're in fighting trim *and* have demonstrated restraint—such as not trying to maim your opponent permanently—I'll get you a human sparring partner. Someone with the suitable skill level and actual combat experience; no point letting you savage a perfectly sheltered civilian."

She pushes herself up so she is straddling Vishrava, her body still thrumming with adrenaline. It does not escape her that to her senses this is hard to distinguish from straddling human with a gorgeous face and breasts that look like they'll fit into her hands just right. Metallic sheen or not. Aloud she says, "Am I some kind of feral beast? Is that what you think?"

"Are you not?" Vishrava places one hand on her hip as if to steady her, though in truth she hardly needs it. "A beautiful beast, red-toothed and gold-eyed, jaw poised to devour. Your appetite would yawn so very wide, yet it'd be such a surgical thing." The hand moves slowly, lightly, in circles.

It is skin hunger, Recadat tells herself, even as that touch burns—a line of fire that pierces her deep, spearing her on its cinderous tip. Like Chun Hyang, Vishrava is not made of nerves and need: xe is cold calculation and honed heuristics. "I'm not your plaything."

"You're on top of me."

She stands so quickly it makes her vertiginous, the sudden altitude change, this dreadful weak body. Vishrava remains on the mat, looking up at her, a little amused and as immaculate as ever—the proxy is not the kind that simulates sweat or even respiration. More statuary than person.

"It is not every day," says the AI, "that I receive a contestant from the Septet game as one of my charges."

Her fingertips turn to icicles. "What about it?"

"The Garden of Atonement cannot help you," Vishrava goes on, "at least not per our dictum. To receive our grace, you must believe yourself capable of redemption—or that you *need* redemption. But I don't think you believe so. To you attempting to destroy Chun Hyang was your greatest act, one that would absolve you of all the killing you did on Septet; it would erase your mistakes and anoint your soul. It would have been your triumph."

She breathes in. She breathes out.

"As far as Ravana and Mahiravanan are concerned, this presented an insurmountable obstacle. How could we guide you to where you need to be, if you feel no guilt? Initially they didn't want to admit you at all." Vishrava rises now, drawing close until xe towers over Recadat. "I disagreed."

Recadat's mouth is dry. She does not allow even one of her fingers to twitch. "Why?"

The AI cups her chin, bending close. Vishrava's eyelashes are long, white with the faintest specks of crimson. "Because you can be changed. *I* can change you. I'm most pleased that you chose me and not either of them. All they would have done is pointlessly break you."

She shivers and fights to remain as she is, to not lean into the AI's body, to not give into this display of warmth—of want. She's made that mistake once with a machine; she will not do so again. "And what's . . . how do you intend to change me?"

Vishrava lowers xer head and brings xer mouth to Recadat's brow. Xer lips move against her skin. A cool hand strokes down her hair, fingernails gliding along her scalp. "This is what will happen. I will fill the hollow places inside you, seal the injuries that still bleed, and put right what has been wronged. I will love you, Recadat, and teach you to love us in return. Finally you will be made whole."

Late afternoon sends her to a class in woodworking, led by Ravana's Beguiling. She feels stupid at first—she has never learned to do anything with her hands. Her degree was in criminology and after graduating she went into public security right away: her evaluations were an excellent match. After that her education was in first aid and techniques in self-defense, in disabling, in killing. In those too she proved adept. Those are the object lessons her hands have learned.

Ravana is patient, despite his apparent misgivings to her admission. He shows her the tools: chisel, handsaw, planes. Each he demonstrates the use and handling of, on blocks and cylinders of fabricated timber. A drone collects the shavings and discarded pieces to recycle into more wood. "They're like weapons, except you use them on wood instead of on people," he tells her, tapping a hand plane. "You should be able to understand that."

She does not, quite, take offense. Some inmates learn in groups. She is allowed to learn alone because, Ravana says, she embarrasses easily. He does not mention why he thinks so: another insight gleaned from her psychological profile. Eventually he leaves her alone with the small hill of materials. There is wood in every color: birch so ashen it resembles clean bone, mahogany in rich fox-red, pine and poplar in pale gold, maple that is between beige and pink. She has never known that wood comes in so many varieties, could be naturally so many hues and shades. Despite the oddity of woodworking in a corrective facility, she finds herself fascinated by the material. The labyrinthine grain, the patterns that make her think of rippling ink, the burls that swirl like fingerprints. Synthetic, as all things in the Garden of Atonement must be, but she's been told they were made with the blueprints of real trunks. Complete fidelity in reproduction, deformities and all.

Her overlays show her directions and suggestions of what she can make, but for a time she's content simply shaping the pieces. She doesn't remove the odd growths, the rough edges and knots: she looks instead for where function could be drawn out of them, could be created in spite of their imperfections. She imagines bookstands, cups, little figurines. Maybe she could make small rough animals, approximations of dogs or fish. The thought amuses her even when it becomes obvious she lacks the skill or the deftness to achieve it—the best she can do is a boxy mass, asymmetrical and barely quadrupedal.

It pleases her to transform the timber, even if her efforts are useless and hideous, and it strikes her that this is the first time she's been able to enjoy this peculiar liberty. To simply sit at leisure and chip away at raw materials; to make something out of nothing. Even the scents of bamboo and hickory and pine soothe her when it's never occurred to her before that wood could have pleasing smells.

When Ceres turns up to fetch her, the woman grimaces and steps gingerly around the shavings. "Ravana indoctrinated you into this? What is with him and woodworking."

Recadat puts her chisel down. Her shoulders and back ache from having bent over the workbench for so long. "It's meditative."

"Now you sound like Zerjic. Docile. You don't really believe what they tell you, do you?"

I will love you, Recadat, and teach you to love us in return. "They can hear us perfectly well."

"They don't care." Ceres motions, her fingernails and knuckles glinting with dabs of luminescent colors: little galaxies. "Their teachings function like a cult's. I suspect it's probably an experiment, to see if they could turn us into biddable little cows. There's a threat of consequences if we step out of line of course, but I've kept pushing the limits. The worst that's ever happened to me was being transferred from Ravana to Vishrava, and that was more a question of fit than it was a punishment."

Recadat straightens all the way up, brushing her hands off. Wood shavings cling to her all over—it is novel, to be dirtied by something she's worked on with her hands rather than by blood, by the muck of city drains drenched by the monsoon and industrial waste, by hunts and treks through fields of black grass. "You won't convince me there is *no* disciplinary action." Zerjic must have been subjected to something.

"Only if you do something drastic—attempted physical or sexual assault, serious damage to Garden of Atonement property, trying to hack into their subsystems. But for anything else, they're pretty lenient. That's the experiment, little girl. Look and sound stern, hint at dark consequences but don't carry them out. They want to see what happens if they manufacture fear. Whether humans can be reduced to trained rats, and so far they must be bored stiff at the result being so predictable. Except for me, I'm the wild variable."

"I've been here for a couple days," Recadat says. "Forgive me if I don't trust everything you say." She doesn't add that she has been in a human-run prison before, and wherever Ceres was kept prior to coming here, it was a softer and gentler place than what Recadat went through.

"You're such a nervous, brittle thing. Vishrava's making you part of xer experiment, either xer own or a piece of the greater puzzle." Ceres steps aside to let Recadat through the door. "Listen, AIs are *not* incomprehensible spirits. They're not gods. They have concrete goals that are actually quite fathomable if you can grasp the usual factors. What benefit they stand to gain. What's the currency they're trading in. Discover those and the rest comes together."

"And you've got it all figured out."

"Nearly." Ceres shrugs—her dress hisses like a nest of snakes suddenly disturbed. "I lived in Shenzhen for a couple years. Let's just say I have some . . . insight into the AI psyche."

The seat of power to the Mandate, the collective to which all AIs belong, even the wardens. A governing body of sorts, responsible for the treaties between machines and humankind. "Is that where you want to go, after here?"

"Oh yes. Our benevolent caretakers can guarantee us entry into Shenzhen Sphere, after we've completed our terms. As fine a home as any—finer than most. There you can live in luxury, if you have the right connections, and Vishrava *is* the right connection." She loosens one pin from her hair, holds it up to Recadat. The point of it glints: brilliant gold, a dot of sunlight. "This is sharp, isn't it. There's enough point to it. You can press it against skin, just so, and it'd go through. An eyeball? Even better. You can do real damage. Yet the wardens let us carry things like these around. What do you think of *that*?"

"It's a temptation. To let us try it, if we dare. And be punished, if we give in." She is familiar with such ploys, and in any case murder may be accomplished with bare hands. The ways by which a person's mortality can collapse are infinite. Weapons merely expedite.

"And it gives an illusion of freedom." Ceres smiles as they turn a corner. The corridors never look quite the same, but she either has a better sense of direction than Recadat or gets better navigation aid in her overlays. "Let's talk about Septet."

She stops walking. "What about it?"

"The world where the Mandate runs their game. Humans pair up with AIs, fight each other to the death, and one winner gets to ask the Mandate for whatever they want. Their greatest desire. Their most impossible fantasy." Ceres meets Recadat's eyes. "You fought there, didn't you? What was your wish? How close did you get to your AI partner?"

"I don't see why I would tell you any of that."

Ceres puts a hand to her heart, eyes widening in mock surprise. "I have information on the Garden of Atonement. You have information on Septet. We could come to a fair deal. I'm curious what the *point* of their game really is."

Recadat knows. She also knows that if she yields any of it she would be executed, Vishrava's promises or not.

When she doesn't answer, Ceres goes on, "It's why you are here, isn't it? Because you lost on Septet. It must have been so humiliating, but at least you escaped with your life, which I understand is more than can be said for most." She continues to smile, her mouth very red, as though she's fresh from a feast of raw, carnivorous succulence. "Shall we get going? Zerjic's slated to sing—eir tessitura is extensive and ey's probably classically trained. I'll play the piano. We'll all entertain Vishrava and xer other charges. Perhaps you could dance or juggle?"

The valve that's been twisting tight in her finds its limit. Recadat slams the woman into the wall, kicking her legs out from under her before Ceres can orient herself. She closes her hand around Ceres' gracile throat, thinks of but stops herself from punching the woman in the gut.

"I'm not your toy," she whispers. "I'm not here to amuse you."

Ceres stares at her, breathing a little hard, and chuckles. "You do have teeth, but I expected you would, it'd be dull otherwise. Nearly murdered an AI, isn't that a feat. They must have done horrible things to you for it."

Recadat backs away. She waits for one of the wardens to instantly materialize and take her away. Or a drone to swoop in and tranquilize her like she is a misbehaving zoo exhibit. No such thing happens.

"Do you see, though?" Ceres is straightening out her dress of black ink-slashes and indigo brushstrokes. "In a normal prison you'd have been electroshocked and put in solitary for what you just did to me. Here, well, the wardens don't think your fangs are real and they likely project you wouldn't do me any real harm. I still don't appreciate being roughed up, but knowing that you have more freedom than you thought, why'd you keep being an obedient drone? Saying what Vishrava wants you to say, doing what Vishrava wants you to do."

"I'll stick to what I am doing. Thank you for your wisdom. Please let Vishrava know I don't have any music or performance skills to offer and won't be joining the group."

"Suits yourself. But it is such a bonding activity." A smirk. "I'm sure xe won't mind. Xe is so lenient with you—such favoritism. Enjoy that while it lasts."

CHAPTER FOUR

Recadat's efforts to wander prove fruitless: most of the facility is closed to her, and she can only access the common areas like the gym or the solarium. Sometimes there aren't even doors, and her overlays indicate what she faces is a blank wall with nothing behind it, but she knows the Garden of Atonement is gigantic. Each inmate, she is sure now, is given different navigation and the corridors shift to block or redirect them as needed.

There's no way for her to meet other inmates outside of the classes and morning orisons—socializing is supervised, strictly regulated. Even the subgroups under each warden's care are segregated, and it doesn't look like she'll be allowed to meet Vishrava's herd outside of Zerjic and Ceres. She understands the methodology; it is about isolating and limiting variables. Which means Vishrava likely anticipated Ceres would provoke her, and that Recadat would respond with violence. Not too far, not enough to be fatal or even to injure. Calculations made within machine margins.

She wonders if it was her self-control that Vishrava counted on or her trauma. Her reflexive terror of what would happen if she bruised or broke Ceres.

In the end she returns to the gym, to watch the water, to imagine herself at sea: adrift, alone. It doesn't occupy her long. She retreats into her overlays, more carefully this time, and discovers the time-traveling show is gone—censored from her access tier, she'd guess. Instead she's nudged toward virtuality programs, perhaps in response to her fixation on the horizon. Several present the obvious: escape to beautiful worlds and gracious cities, simulation of the lives of celebrities and heroes—pirate captains, politicians, actors of intergalactic fame. Various erotic scenarios are available, of different levels of explicitness, aided by preset artificial lovers.

One program is simply called *Qualia*. It requests access to remnant data: she doesn't know what that means, and her search yields no useful answers from the Garden's libraries. Impulsively she grants access, and the program pulls her under.

A bar. Smoked quartz countertop, dim lighting, glasses overhead like warped fruits.

"Slow day," the person seated next to her says. "In our line of work though, I've come to appreciate slow days. What about you?"

She snaps around. Thannarat is as she remembers: broad-shouldered and dark-skinned, a face with the stern features of a wolf, dressed in the bulky armored coat she wore everywhere. Armed, one visible holster and another hidden. She was never a woman content to carry only a single gun. One large hand is clasped around a cup of cold sake, the ceramic dainty between her thick fingers.

"You," Recadat whispers. "You're dead."

Thannarat smiles. The same smile—a twist of the mouth. It looks cruel even when Thannarat does not mean it to. "Is that a fact? I've missed you, old partner. It has been so long."

A patron passes by, hurrying toward the exit. They are faceless, a thin wraith. "You're just a ghost." Remnant data, that is what it means, harvested from the stems that once held her neural implants; that are alive again, resurrected by the new implants Ravana installed. Necromantic exo-memory.

"I'm exactly what I appear to be, my tiger." She pours a second cup and slides it toward Recadat. "Been taking care of yourself much? You always treated food and sleep as optional, but you're still human."

"Thannarat." Her throat closes. "You're not real. You died on Septet." So Recadat could live.

"Did I, now." Thannarat stands—she is imposing, has more than thirty centimeters over Recadat. She fetches another bottle from behind the bar, vodka this time, the bottle luminescent: tiny holograms blur across the surface. "How did that happen exactly? I like to think I'm harder to kill than most."

"There was—" She does not know why she is doing this, explaining to a ghost the minutiae of its death, a ghost that is nothing more than a recreation harvested from her own memories. Her eyes are hot. "Chun Hyang's Glaive pierced you. The game was called to a draw and I was allowed to leave. Your AI couldn't protect you." Neither could Recadat.

Her old partner looks at her. "I see. That's unfortunate. Not much I can do about it, I suppose. Hope I made a picturesque corpse. What happened to it, anyway?"

"I had it collected and sent to Ayothaya, the ashes buried in our home city, at a spot where you can see the river." This comes out automatically, but when she pauses she realizes that is not quite right. After Septet, she bent herself to revenge, to Chun Hyang's annihilation. There was no time or opportunity for that send-off. But it seems close enough. She takes a deep breath. "Are you . . . going to persist? Can I come back to this and see you every time?" Tears threaten. She swallows them back.

"Most likely." Thannarat's hand passes through her as though one or both of them is smoke. Her fingers press against Recadat's—she sees now that it is she who is the phantom, translucent next to the solidity that is Thannarat. "I need you to remember, Recadat."

She tries to ask what it is that she's supposed to remember, but already the simulation is fading. Qualia informs her that it has reached the limit of remnant data, that what is there is insufficient for a further reconstruction at this time. At this time—she is back on the pool's edge, shaking.

When she looks up, she finds she's not alone.

Thannarat stands at the other end of the pool—or rather at the other end of the illusion, within the projected sea and horizon. She blinks. The image remains, black-coated and facing the sun, silhouetted against a distant imaginary shore.

Recadat doesn't think. She wades in. Once she'd have been swift: now she's constrained by the limitations of weak flesh, weak muscles, but she moves as fast as she can even as the water resists and rises. Now to her waist, now to her chest.

She is almost at the far end when Zerjic grabs her from behind, lifting her bodily out of the water. "Can you actually swim?"

"Yes." She licks her mouth—salt has crusted on her lips. The apparition has vanished.

"You didn't look like you were going to swim; you looked like you were going to drown yourself."

Ey drags her out of the pool; she does not resist. They both drip onto the gym's floor, which absorbs the water as quickly as it falls. Like thirsty soil, or like the floor of a hospital. Her skin is icy.

"At the deepest end, the pool's two meters. You're not even a hundred seventy, buoyancy or not." Zerjic is holding onto her tight as though ey thinks she might break free and dive back into the water. "Listen, if you're suicidal then I need to tell Vishrava about it. I don't know why xe isn't keeping more of an eye on you."

She does not want to deal with the warden. Not right now. "I'm not suicidal. I'll prove it."

Her footing is unsteady but she makes do, using eir shoulders as handholds as she kisses em on the mouth. Eir lips are full and soft, so unlike the hard planes of eir other features, eir body furnace-hot next to the cold saltwater. Eir teeth graze against her lips. Eir tongue slips into her mouth, flicking, testing.

They pull apart. "Come to my room," Zerjic says, voice thick.

As simple as that, as impetuous. She follows; ey leads her by the hand, a gesture that is almost adolescent in sweetness, intimate in its certainty. Recadat expects to be stopped—a rule against inmates fraternizing—but no one impedes them in the short walk to Zerjic's room.

Eir arrangement is dominated by indigo, by panels of black relieved by glimmers of cobalt. But she does not have long to survey and appreciate the décor—Zerjic pushes her up against the wall, with much different intentions this time, and pins one of her wrists over her head. Ey slips one hand into her shirt, pinching a nipple already hard.

She clutches at the back of eir skull with her free hand and kisses em again, this time harder, more carnivorous. Her thighs part for em and ey slips in a finger, two fingers, eir thumb circling and rubbing and making lights scintillate behind her eyelids. She thinks of another person, and then doesn't think at all as she scrabbles for purchase, wrapping one leg around Zerjic's waist. She jerks and arches; she ruts. Her nerves become a chorus.

It ends. She hangs boneless in Zerjic's arms, tender as a new wound, as full as she is hollowed out. Whether she made sounds during all this she does not remember.

"You're very beautiful." Zerjic's tongue traces the shell of her ear. Eir fingers are still in her, lightly crooked. "Ever since Vishrava brought you in, I've been wanting to try you. You looked such a feral little thing."

Recadat palms eir chest, realizing that ey has not taken off even a single stitch of clothing. The thought pricks her with a new frisson of desire. "You must've tried everyone else."

"Jealous?" Ey steers her toward the bed, where ey lays her down and strips off her trousers. Ey bends to strokes her calf, to kiss her thigh. A thumb plays with her pubic hair. "Ceres is not my type, if that is what you're worrying about. Too petulant, and anyway she'd rather sleep with the wardens."

"Has she?" She almost asks *Have you?* but thinks better of it.

"Probably. She is persistent and some of the wardens are indulgent—it could be part of her rehabilitation. Why talk about her, though, she's so irrelevant. Let us talk about you." Ey rises, not quite straddling her, eir weight balanced on eir hands and knees. "You fell into my arms like you fell into an old habit. Who do I remind you of?"

No one, Recadat considers saying. Yet it all spills out of her anyway, because she needs to tell it to someone—a confessional, a lancing of the suppurative wound. "Her name was Thannarat. She was about your build."

"Large?" Zerjic suggests.

"Larger. Taller than you by ten centimeters or so, a little broader. She took up space wherever she went, and people thought she was rough. But it was just the way she looked. Wolfish. Hungry. And she was those things, but she was more . . . " Kind, when she chose to be. Recadat thinks of the single kiss they shared at dawn, mere hours before Thannarat's demise.

"You were lovers."

"Not really." They did not get the chance. "She and I used to be colleagues before that, and then we—I supposed it was a little predictable."

Ey smirks down at her. "So you have a type."

Recadat takes hold of em, pulls them onto the bed beside her. Zerjic laughs and cups her body with eirs. "Have you met anyone in here that resembles her description?"

"Is she likely to have wound up here?"

Thannarat is dead. She is fairly sure of that. But then she is not quite. That ghost in Qualia. The indistinct shades of her own memory. The tortures in the human-run prison that left blank patches in her mind, pockets of buzzing whiteness. "I saw someone who looked like her in the solarium. A lot like her."

"I don't think I would have forgotten someone like that." Ey raises an eyebrow. "And reuniting you with my sexual competition seems like self-sabotage, but . . . There are two groups of inmates I haven't seen much of: several of Ravana's brides and a group of Mahiravanan's votaries who receive their regimen in seclusion. The latter is impossible to reach. The former, maybe."

It occurs to Recadat to ask why ey is helping her at all, then she realizes ey has not offered help yet—not really. She turns to face Zerjic and kisses eir throat.

Ey lets her get eir clothing out of the way enough for her to lick and nibble her way down eir hard stomach. A sheen of sweat alloys the planes of eir flesh; she tastes that too.

She continues until her head is between eir legs and her mouth is fastened to em, to eir hot pulsing nerves. She tends and works and laps until ey quakes around her, above her. Hard thighs clench against her ears. Ey fills her mouth and she swallows.

Later Zerjic holds her in eir arms—the sentimental sort, she thinks, a surprise—and lays eir hand on her belly, making slow circles with eir fingers. Eir breath tickles her nape. "You've made me curious. I'll see if I can lure some of the brides out, or cajole one into talking to me at any rate."

People are transactional, she learned that in prison. Zerjic as much as anyone else, weighing cost and benefit, the worth of carnal pleasure—the value her body can offer. She settles against em, all the same: she was the one who began this. And in the dim lighting of Zerjic's room it is not so difficult to pretend she is with another. It is not so difficult to pretend she is with Thannarat.

❧

The next morning she is in the gym, under Vishrava's guidance: exercises to pinpoint where she's gone weak, to regain strength, to bring back her flexibility. "You used to have musculoskeletal augmentation," xe is saying after she's finished her stretches. "We could look into replacing it. Ravana is an excellent surgeon."

Recadat doesn't think much of being operated on by an AI who didn't even want her here. "You wouldn't do it?" Not that she trusts Vishrava more, but xe at least voted to admit her.

"He is the one with the expertise." Vishrava helps her to her feet. "Why, do you think each AI can execute all things perfectly?"

"I was under the impression. Yes." She keeps her tone careful. "Most humans are."

Xe strokes her hand, thumb gliding along her palm. "Each AI has their own parameters, the same as any human. We are guided by the base of our genesis, and so we have predilections, preferences, specialties. I'd be able to operate on you as well as an average human surgeon, but you want an exceptional one."

"On Shenzhen machines are holy."

Vishrava laughs, tossing xer albino curls. "In the Garden of Atonement we are the same, but not to you, I'm sure. The Septet game can have such a drastic impact on human opinion of us, usually for the worse. It's one reason why I personally don't care for it, even though I've been invited to participate before. But we'll sit down to discuss your cybernetics later, there are military-grade ones available if you're interested in those—actually what we have is quite a bit better. I want to give you anything that makes you feel secure."

"Then why do you let humans staff the Shenzhen detention

orbital?" The question tumbles out of her almost without her volition. But there's no taking it back.

"It fulfills a doctrinal function in AI-human relations, and the personnel get to feel they're in control of *something*. Again, I disapprove. Even your sentence in there I'd have commutated if I could—the world does not learn by brutality. Chun Hyang was being a sadist." Xe hands her a towel. "Now, about Zerjic."

Recadat concentrates on wiping herself dry. Sweat clings like icicles to her skin. "What about em?"

"Fraternizing happens, of course, and we allow it because sometimes it can be good for our charges—the sense of connection, the bond; it even lasts beyond the Garden of Atonement on occasion. But I need to know if you were coerced in any way."

Zerjic's mouth on hers, velvet and hungry. "Did I look coerced?"

"No. It's necessary for me to be sure, regardless. You should speak to me if any of your . . . assignations are less than enthusiastic." Vishrava cants xer long torso. "I can pilot a proxy more to your tastes."

Her cheeks warm. "There's no need."

"As you like. Shall we spar?"

It is both harder and easier this time: Vishrava no longer treats her like a beginner, but she's surer and more limber, and she's given a knife. By the end of it she has collected one hit that'll bloom into a bruise. She hardly minds—it means more than anything to feel in control of her body again and, she realizes, even sex with Zerjic serves that end. An exchange, yes, but also because she desires it. Her volition and her body's use align. Despite her misgivings, she thinks of asking for that operation. If the wardens wish to make modifications she didn't consent to, they already would have. And she wants to feel strength coursing through her again. Before all this she never had many augmentations, but even the basic ones that enhance metabolism and regulate neurotransmitters . . .

Two inmates enter. They are dressed identically, in bodysuits the color of mulch: a green so deep it nears black, the shade of hidden jungles. Both have the direct, sharp gazes of hawks. Their eyes skim over Vishrava and Recadat, taking note then moving on. Their movements are in perfect sync—even when they stretch and exercise they mirror each other. Recadat watches, growing more disturbed by the minute. Complete tandem, utter harmony as they slip into the pool.

"Ravana's brides," Vishrava tells her. "Gawking is rude. Come—I'll take you to Zerjic."

As though she's a child who can be pacified by promises that she'll get extra time with her favorite playmate. But she would sooner suffer this infantilization than what happened to her in the other prison.

In the lounge, Zerjic is singing to an audience: a Vishrava proxy and several inmates she's never seen before, the latter guarded by a Mahiravanan proxy. Ceres is at the piano, playing as though the keys are her mortal enemies and the instrument has committed an unspeakable affront; she is producing good sound despite that. Recadat chooses a seat and soon realizes that Zerjic is singing simultaneously in tenor and mezzo-soprano. An implant that gives em more than one voice, though the secondary output—a second mouth perhaps—isn't immediately visible. Ey is dressed in an asymmetric shirt, ombre gray-to-black, one arm sleeveless. It bares the hard beauty of eir bicep, where dermals glisten in fine gold webs, accentuating each line of muscle. A metal snake curls around eir forearm, covering eir wrist and the back of eir hand.

The duet ey sings is tragic: lovers sundered, sudden violence, great calamities. Recadat tries not to think of parallels to her life and instead makes herself focus on eir voice—the sonorous tones, the one-person duet. There's power in it, silk and suede, and ey has obviously been schooled. She wonders at eir background, at the sort of education that included classical music and which led em to integrate uncommon vocal implants. It is not a pretense, not something Zerjic has adopted to make emself interesting or useful to Vishrava. Ey is radiant in song, ennobled by it, made transcendent by music.

The performance ends. Applause follows—some for politeness, some out of sincerity. Recadat finds herself clapping in earnest. Mahiravanan's inmates leave with their warden. Ceres straightens from the piano, brushing off her hands. She watches Recadat approach Zerjic with a knowing little smirk.

"Little lovebirds," she says as she draws close to them. "I can't believe you would choose a human lover over a machine."

Zerjic's expression doesn't change. Neither does Vishrava's, whose two proxies are folding the furniture into the floor and tidying the piano, performing busywork.

Then Zerjic smiles and slides one arm around Recadat's waist. "My charms work on beautiful women on occasion, Ceres. Is that so hard to credit?"

Ceres raises an eyebrow. "Indulge me, Zerjic. I'd like to spar."

"After the piano?"

"The piano always puts me in a mood. And your singing. Excellent, of course, but it makes one carnivorous—unless you and Recadat are in haste to adjourn elsewhere?"

Ey laughs, slides one hand up Recadat's spine, and then lets go. "I can control myself, though presently it is a challenge. Well, let's get to it." Ey unwraps the bracelet from eir arm and hands it to Recadat. "Keep an eye on this for me, will you?"

The piece is serpent-headed, its scaled, flexible body forming the bracelet. Black metal, lightly textured. She hefts it in her hand: dense and heavy. The head seems to thrum beneath the surface, its red eyes slowly pulsing.

Ceres passes her hand over the front of her dress. It folds and contracts, sleeves and skirt reshaping, until it fits her like a body sheath. Zerjic leaves eir attire be, though ey sheds eir waistcoat and hangs it neatly on one of the few chairs Vishrava has not put away. The warden's proxies sit down to watch. Recadat grows more certain that she is in a madhouse.

Against her expectations, Ceres fights like a boxer: the high guard, the quick jabs. Zerjic out-bulks her but moves lightly, staying out of reach, intending to evade until she's tired out. But Ceres is aggressive—she pursues across the floor, striking with bruising force. Recadat judges her speed and vigor: in her prime, she'd be able to take Ceres. Not at the present. It galls her, but she knows her current limits.

She sees Zerjic's opening the same time Ceres does, and Ceres takes it running.

Ceres tackles em to the floor, jabbing at eir face, pulling the blow at the last moment. Her grin is wide and red.

In the next minute, Zerjic bucks and throws Ceres off. Ey springs to eir feet, weightless, nearly balletic. Pure element of surprise as ey twists around and shoves Ceres into the wall face-first. Ey pins her arms behind her and closes eir hand around her neck—Recadat catches a glimpse of eir expression: remote as a glacier. "Yield," Zerjic says.

Vishrava stands and claps xer hands. "That will suffice."

They separate. Zerjic fetches eir waistcoat and puts it back on; ey has rearranged eir expression to its amused neutrality, urbane, absent any thought of violence—the face of someone who cannot possibly have just done what ey did, let alone so efficiently. Ceres' mouth is a tight, furious line.

Recadat returns the bracelet to em as the two of them exit the lounge. "I don't know why Ceres tried that," ey says once they're in the corridor and well out of Ceres' earshot. "She knows what I can do."

She falls into step beside em, tamping down the urge to touch eir bicep: to feel the tautness of it, the fine ridges of golden dermals. "What did you really do before you came here?"

"Field mercenary." Ey makes a little shrug. "All things considered, I don't mind telling you—it's not like it isn't obvious I was a combatant. Anyway, none of Mahiravanan's acolytes was your woman, I take it?"

Ey was watching for her reaction during eir performance. "They weren't."

"I'll ask for a bigger audience next time. Say a few dozen—that's good for my ego." Ey slides the bracelet back on, the cobra's head resting on top of eir wrist, the rest of it expanding and contracting until it settles against eir forearm. "Will take us a while to go through them this way, but we have time. Don't suppose you could play an instrument?"

"No." She tries not to grimace or admit that she never had a hobby. "You're going out of your way for me."

"I told you—I'm curious. And when I pursue something, I don't let go until it's concluded to my satisfaction."

Something in the cadence of eir voice—the way it drops, the way it glimmers with intent—goes through her like sudden fever. "What are you doing after this?" she asks inanely, already suspecting the answer.

Zerjic locks eyes with her. Eir smile is slow. "You." Ey lifts her hand, turns it, presses eir lips to her pulse-point. "Adrenaline's an aphrodisiac. Don't you think?"

"You didn't get an adrenaline rush out of mocking Ceres."

"No," ey concedes. "I got one out of you watching. Out of you knowing I fought in your honor. Didn't you feel it, that little thrill, that spark?"

Recadat doesn't bother answering a rhetorical question. She grabs eir collar, pulls em in. They kiss like knives. She tastes the hot copper of eir blood.

Zerjic licks eir mouth as ey draws back—the first to break contact. "If we were anywhere else, I'd take you right now. Right here."

Her fists are clenched tight in eir waistcoat. "What's stopping you."

"The wardens won't be impressed. Vishrava considers public sex a disturbance to other inmates. Really kills spontaneity." Ey runs eir hand down her flank, her stomach, as though ey can't wait to strip her. "Your room or mine?"

"Yours." Irrational: her room does not seem hers. Vishrava has been there too often. No doubt xe has been in Zerjic's as much.

This time she leads, impatiently tugging em along. Ey chuckles low in eir throat.

The door to eir room has barely shut when ey tears her clothes off, not as roughly as she wants, but enough that it risks the seams splitting, the fabric ripping. She doesn't get the opportunity to fall into eir bed—ey lifts her with incredible strength and throws her onto the sheets.

Recadat lands, bare and gasping, her skin goosing from the cold. Ey has removed eir bracelet. It coils, mobile as a real serpent, in eir hand.

"How much," ey says, "do you trust me in bed?"

"Completely." Stupid, but at this moment she's not entirely thinking with her cerebral parts.

"Safeword?"

"Sturnidae." Recadat doesn't quite know where that came from—something used with previous partners? But it comes easily, and works well enough.

A flicker crosses Zerjic's expression, but ey then grips both her wrists in one practiced hand. With the other ey wraps the bracelet around, makeshift restraint, the piece of jewelry tightening until it is as definite as manacles.

Her cardiac muscles jackknife. Do everything to me, she wants to say, give me everything I did not have before. Ey is a near-stranger, and yet.

"If only you could see yourself. Bound for me, all of you surrendered and pliant." Zerjic's face is beatific as ey descends upon her. "A feast."

She shivers but ey doesn't take her mouth. Instead ey lavishes her throat with attention, soft nibbling then hungrier bites. Lightning arcs across her nerves when ey sinks eir teeth in like a snare clenching shut. Her nails claw at the bracelet, but she does nothing to stop or dislodge em; all of her is being razed with slow fire, with this act of deliberate consumption.

"I thought you were going to tear up my throat," she says when ey lets go. In another lifetime she said to Thannarat, *You look like you'd snap your jaw around a beautiful woman's throat and tear her open, and she'd thank you for it.*

Zerjic licks eir lips. "If you ask me nicely. And if we have the right first aid on hand."

The thought of her throat dressed, wearing for days the evidence of what ey has done to her. Recadat tries to meter her inhalation, her exhalation. She forces her hands to still in their cage of black steel and cobra's head. "Give me the rest," she says, her breath serrating against her mouth. "The rest of you. The rest of what you want to do to me." Until she is a single enormous wound, bleeding for eir delight.

"Demanding." Ey thumbs where ey has left prints of eir teeth. A delicious ache answers. "Don't worry. I'll take care of you well and thoroughly."

Nevertheless ey takes eir time. Stroking her, exploring her: her breasts hefted, her stomach licked, tantalizing contact on her inner thighs. The air remains cold—ey has not adjusted the temperature—but she feels like a furnace being stoked to life. Ey arranges her to eir convenience, now on her back, now on her side. As if she is a sculpture, fresh-made, that ey personally planned and sketched and brought to life. Every dimension eirs to possess and peruse. Pygmalion and Galatea, that Hellenic story.

When Zerjic wraps eir mouth around her nipple, she jolts. Then again when ey curves eir palm over her other breast and wet warmth closes around that too. Eir second mouth, concealed before by the bracelet that—she thinks with her last few shreds of coherence—must have acted as an amplifier for eir extra voice.

Ey lifts eir head to look at her. The second mouth continues in its attentions. "What do you think?" As though daring her to be repulsed by an implant so unusual.

Recadat rasps, "Yes."

A chuckle that vibrates against her skin. Ey seeks between her legs with the implanted hand, parting her with scalpel precision. Eir fingers plunge inside her, no resistance at all, and the second mouth latches onto her clitoris. It is not a perfect analogue to the conventional mouth but it is close, the tongue longer and more dexterous. She makes harsh helpless sounds, pushing against eir wrist, urging em deeper.

Ey muzzles her with eir lips. She writhes. Zerjic's tongue in her mouth, as though ey means to penetrate her in every way, enter her through every available gate. Climax arrives like the tide: successive, relentless. Ey doesn't let up until she is entirely limp, shuddering weakly, her voice hoarse in her throat.

Zerjic withdraws eir hand, every finger glistening; she catches a glimpse of the mouth, a thin line that nearly disappears into the base of eir palm. Ey unties her. Recadat flexes her fingers—less numb than she'd expect, her skin marked by fine crosshatching, slightly red.

"You're very good," she says, an understatement.

"The best you've ever had?" Smug. Teasing.

"Yes." Even Chun Hyang cannot compare, for all their machine precision.

Ey grins, now. "Better than your true love?"

"We never—" Recadat turns aside, nearly away from em. "I told you that."

The smile dissolves. "You did. I'm sorry—my competitive streak got the best of me. It was . . . not right, when you don't even know if she can be found again."

Or even if Thannarat is alive. "It doesn't matter."

"Of course it matters. I don't want to upset you, not now or ever."

She covers her face with one hand, breathing slowly through. "You don't have to." Be this kind. This caring, or a good appearance of it. She's so weak that eir gentleness pierces her without effort. Once she defended herself better, built an entire fortress around her soul. The only person who ever got through was—

"Zerjic." Recadat lets her hand drop.

Ey blinks. "You're sounding very serious. Was it something I said?"

"Have you used Qualia?"

"The meditative virtuality? Vishrava told me to try it once, so I did, but I can't say it suits me."

Recadat moves to explain, that it is where the ghost of Thannarat abides, the ghost of the only person who's ever made her feel human. But it sounds demented and she doesn't want to appear any more unstable to em than she already does. "It's nothing," she says. "Nothing at all."

CHAPTER FIVE

In the end Zerjic takes off most of eir clothes so ey can lie skin-to-skin with Recadat. Ey seldom does that with a new lover, but Recadat is special in more ways than one. When Zerjic presses eir bare chest to her back, the last tension in her body drains away and she settles against em, calming into deep sleep.

Ey's always had a weakness for this, for watching a lover at rest. And she is beautiful in repose, the only time ey's seen this woman so tranquil. What has been done to her ey has some idea of, and ey has not pressed for detail. Learn too much and sympathy will blunt em. Ey's more invested than ey should be as it is.

When Recadat arrived, Zerjic already had a suspicion; the codeword *Sturnidae* confirms it—that this is the package ey's been waiting for. Of necessity contained in a human body, there was nothing else that could have entered this place undetected. Now all ey has to do is keep her alive until she completes her work, and after that she will become the altar-sacrifice while Zerjic secures eir exit. Though by then, if all goes well, extraction will be as simple as walking out and slipping into a suitable ship.

Ey looks down at her. Grimaces. In retrospect ey should have asked the Ministry of Deficit Control to send a mule that wouldn't be eir type—a man would have been easy to treat as the lamb on the chopping block. But then the ministry chief knows ey would have been less motivated to get close.

Zerjic lightly strokes Recadat's stomach, feeling the sharpness of ribs there. Once there must have been more fat and much more muscle. Former police, and former participant in the Septet game. Brought low and shattered by the latter. Briefly ey speculates what this woman was like before all this happened to her; what she will be like if she is healed.

All that is foolish. Ey's getting attached. What ey will need to do is to let her saturate the Garden of Atonement's network with the isotoxal virus, then ey will activate what she has sown, and run. Home awaits, and more besides when ey returns in victory.

Recadat turns, wrapping one arm around em, muttering in her sleep. Ey doesn't catch it—likely the name of her lost love, the syllables are about right. The wisps of her hair—some the bright green of starling pinions—stir under Zerjic's breath. Ey does not consider emself soft or easily ensnared, let alone by a woman who would not give back the fullest of what ey has to offer. But ey knows eir vices. A certain fragility; the brittleness that wars with ferocity. Ey wonders what she'd look like in real combat.

A notification. Ey disentangles from Recadat, carefully so as not to wake her, and throws on eir clothes.

Vishrava is waiting for her in the corridor, in a proxy more adorned than usual. Jeweled cheekbones, mermaid scales on xer throat and breasts, a temptation brought up from the deep. "Zerjic," xe says. "I trust the two of you have had a mutually restorative time."

Ey smiles. Controlling eir expression has always come easily to em, even if the warden's phrasing turns eir stomach. "Did you need me for anything?"

The AI nods, pleased the way xe would be with an obedient pet, a tame child. "In point of fact, yes. I'm due to receive an honored guest. She has particular tastes, and I'd like you to distract her so that she doesn't splash around too much damage."

An odd order. "How much distraction?"

"I don't anticipate she will stay long. It shouldn't be onerous—she is considered a beauty—and of course I won't make you do anything you don't want to. No need to tidy yourself," xe adds. "She will enjoy the disheveled look."

Odder still. Ey assumes the visitor can only be another machine, but Vishrava speaks of her like she's a human—which seems impossible, unless it's a new intake. But xe would not bring an inmate to meet one of those.

Vishrava leads the way to the solarium. It is empty—xe must have ordered other inmates out.

The guest who walks through the door is not a new intake; she moves too easily, too proudly. Not an AI's proxy, Zerjic judges, based on how she carries herself. Something in her bearing speaks of habit and history, which machines don't evince in their physical presentations. Middling height, shorter than Zerjic, clad in a dress whose upper half armors her in tessellated chitin. The lower half falls straight and heavy in a skirt of daggers, in amber and seared red.

"I was told to come see one of the wardens here," says the guest. "You'd be the Wisdom of Vishrava?"

"Yes." Vishrava gestures toward one of the ground-level enclosures. "Welcome to the Garden of Atonement."

"I'm Krissana Khongtip, the human half of this haruspex." The woman holds up her arm: her dress ripples and flows, hardening into a gauntlet tipped in talons. "Oh, I've always wanted to introduce myself like that, it sounds so . . . official. It makes me feel so respectable and potent, like declaring your military rank. I'm sorry to turn up on such short notice. My AI half is Benzaiten in Autumn and xe loves xer little pranks. Not to worry though, you'll be talking to me and I am very serious, not given to mischief at all."

"It's the highest pleasure to receive Benzaiten." Vishrava motions and the floor produces a set of furniture: three tall seats, a low crescent-shaped table. "I'd have thought xe would discuss what xe requires of me xerself."

"Maybe xe wants a change of pace or maybe xe's busy with something else." Krissana lowers her hand: the gauntlet recedes, returns to being the sleeve of an haute couture dress. "You're not in trouble. Xe is just curious, academically. So am I, I'd never heard of the Garden of Atonement until last week or so. Do you mind if I look around?"

"Certainly not, honored haruspex. In fact I'm providing you with a guide." Vishrava nods at Zerjic. "Ey will show you our facilities and answer any questions you may have."

"So kind," Krissana murmurs. "Is ey dangerous?"

"Only if you want me to be," Zerjic says lightly.

Krissana laughs, the sound high and sparkling. Her range lilts toward mezzo-soprano. “Then I must take you up on it. By the way, Vishrava, you don’t have pre-haruspices here, do you?”

“Naturally not. That is reserved for Shenzhen alone.” The warden bows with an archaic flourish. “Please, enjoy yourself.”

In the warden’s absence, Krissana appraises Zerjic with naked curiosity. She looks over the state of eir dress, traces the planes of eir features, surveying all of em as though ey is a map to a country she means to dismantle and conquer. “I’m about to be very frank,” she says. “I can’t help noticing that you look and smell like you’ve just had sex.”

Ey gives her a smile designed for a woman like this: slow, a challenge. The way one dangles a prime cut before a hungry lynx. “Yes. Vishrava dragged me out of bed. I usually dress a lot neater.”

Krissana’s eyes widen as she follows Zerjic toward one of the recreational halls. “So sorry that I interrupted.”

Zerjic thinks of Recadat in bed, the tender portrait of her. Ey hopes she is asleep still, at complete peace, and that ey’ll be back before she wakes up. Abruptly ey does not want her to be alone. “It’s nothing. And Vishrava’s assigned me a perfectly lovely task.”

“Xe must know my tastes.” The haruspex smirks. “It wouldn’t have worked on Benzaiten, so Vishrava anticipated I’d be doing the talking and not my AI half. Do you know what a haruspex is?”

“I have some idea. I should like to hear it from you—I can’t say I’ve ever met one.”

“A haruspex, like me, is a human whose body has been altered and prepared to host an AI. Two souls, one body, insofar as you count an AI as a soul. It can be a convenient arrangement. You can ask Vishrava about it, though of course there should be no haruspices here.” Krissana leans toward em. “You’re one of the Garden of Atonement’s . . . clients, aren’t you? How are you liking the place?”

They have stopped before a gate leading to one of Mahiravanan’s shrines. “The food’s fantastic—we do need to cook sometimes but I hardly mind—and the accommodation is gracious. It’s a little like a holiday. What’s there to complain about?”

Krissana’s mouth pulls into a sickle grin. “A perfectly proper answer. This project's been going on for, let's see, five years, ten months, and twenty-seven days. It's an interesting concept, though I can't say I agree with the methods. Redemption has to come from within, hasn't it."

Ey holds the door open for her. "That's a little too philosophical for me."

The shrine holds a Mahiravanan proxy that assumes the pose of the reclining Buddha. Its eyes follow Krissana and Zerjic, but it neither moves nor speaks. Within the golden folds of its robes, inmates curl up, fetal, or sprawl naked while whispering mantras into the fabric. A couple meditate, bleeding from lacerations across their arms and faces and backs. Zerjic scans the faces, though ey knows Recadat's lover would not be among them anyway—has never been in the Garden of Atonement, whatever else Recadat may have seen. A consequence of the conditioning and rearranged neural stacks.

Krissana pinches her mouth. "This is all . . . very. Tell me, Khun Zerjic, do you find all this helpful and rehabilitative? Or do you find it a little sick?"

Mahiravanan offers no counter. Vishrava is not sending Zerjic any script on how to respond to Krissana. "I'm not one of Mahiravanan's, so I wouldn't know." Ey shrugs, as though the sight before both of them is perfectly normal. "Vishrava's program is different."

"I could ask for you, inform Vishrava you struck my fancy so much I'd like to take you with me as my plaything. Being one with Benzaiten affords me a lot of perks."

"Under normal circumstances, I'd never turn down a proposal from a woman as gorgeous as you. But for reasons of personal ethics, I'd like to complete my terms here." To finish eir mission.

Krissana gives her a quick, wry look. "The woman you just left in bed, is she very beautiful?"

"All my lovers," ey says solemnly, "are beautiful to me."

"Silver-tongued. It really is a shame you won't leave with me. Go on, what else does Vishrava want me to see?"

Their next stop, per Vishrava's steering of Zerjic's navigation, is one of the seclusion chambers for Ravana's brides. Ey wonders if this is intended as an answer to Recadat's search—Vishrava surveils xer inmates' every move and would have listened in on eir pillow talk with Recadat—and this is the first time ey's gotten so close to Ravana's inner cloister.

The hall is low-lit, the ceiling draped in projected clouds. Late dusk, teetering on the edge of true night. Muted music and birdcalls. The brides lie entwined, asleep or mid-coitus; several are having or being had by Ravana proxies. Some are loud. Others make nearly no sound. None of them pause at the sight of visitors.

Exiting, Krissana remarks merely, "Well, I suppose *that* is more therapeutic. In sheer quantity, that's the most . . . interspecies sex I've ever seen in one place. Do you participate?"

"I prefer to be more private. And I don't favor machines."

"Not one for orgies, then." The haruspex fingers the pendant at her throat, a rose-gold cylinder embedded with auroral diamonds. "Then again neither am I, it's too logistically involved. Three partners, at most. My wife, myself, someone honey-mouthed and handsome we ensnared as a gift to one another . . . "

Zerjic checks their last destination. "You don't have much inhibition, do you?"

"None," Krissana says cheerfully. "Within about five minutes of meeting someone, I know whether I want them in bed and if I do, I strive my level best to get them there. I'm an honest woman. Embarrassment is a waste of everyone's time."

Amusement tugs at eir mouth. "I can respect that."

Last they turn to a wide hall that ey knows well: far above are viewports from which spectators may observe, though everyone in the garden must watch the feed in any case when there's anything going on here. For the moment it looks unremarkable, the ground flat and the ceiling unadorned, a few columns here and there bearing projected bas-reliefs of running animals. Clean, unstained by gore. When Krissana asks, Zerjic says only, "This is the ground for evening prayers."

As though that explains everything or as though she knows precisely what it means, she responds with a thoughtful nod. "Well,

I've seen enough. I will take my leave shortly, after chatting with the wardens a little more. Thanks for the tour, Khun Zerjic. I hope you remain in excellent health."

❧

Recadat is half-aware when a connection triggers and Qualia seeps into her overlays like ink in water. She does not stop it, for all that she knows it should not be doing this, should not be able to infiltrate her brain without her volunteering access.

But it is like being drawn into a dream she has been chasing. A perfect dream of a perfect day.

An orchard, this time. The noon pours down, liquid, and the shimmering grass is so soft that it undulates with electrum light as she passes through. The day warms the back of her neck and ears, and her limbs feel strong, full of grace. Years younger, transported to the time before her attempt on Chun Hyang and her prison sentence.

Someone waits for her beneath a tree of green-and-brass leaves and boughs heavy with rose apples. Some are natural peridot and ruby, others are more peculiar cultivars: shades of seafoam and bruise. Thannarat is holding several in her hands, eating them slowly. Glimpses of her teeth, white and sharp, raking through fruit. Self-consciously Recadat reaches to touch her throat, where Zerjic's teeth marks would be, but they haven't carried over into virtuality. Here she is a clean slate.

"I don't actually like rose apples," Thannarat is saying as she draws near. "I like things with more taste. Sweeter, tarter. These don't even have the courtesy of being flavored hybrids. What have you been up to, Recadat?"

There is, Recadat realizes, a softness to the ghost that the living woman never had, diffuse next to the solidity of the real thing. "Not much. I'm in a sort of prison. Corrective facility."

A low chuckle, rumbling in the back of Thannarat's throat. "Whatever could you have done? You're so law-abiding. Perfect moral compass, untarnished by the universe's ills."

"I tried to avenge you."

Thannarat's expression changes. "Why?"

At this she's at a loss. "I loved you." The ghost must remember that; it can't possibly forget what *Recadat* knows—she's already accepted that this is a fantasy cobbled together by records in her overlays and her fantasies. "And you . . . "

"Yes?"

"Didn't you love me?" An echo of a different conversation, herself saying things she can only half-remember. *Thannarat, I've always . . . I never wanted anyone else. You were my war god.* It comes back to her piecemeal. Something about it does not align but she can't place what, or why.

Recadat, please. A gunshot.

The ghost simply smiles. "Of course I do. Not in the past tense, either. I need you to do something for me."

"Yes. Anything." The bite of desperation in her own voice. But she's stopped caring about her own dignity.

"Come back here." Thannarat takes her hand, blunt fingers stroking her palm, climbing up her wrist. "Every chance you get. Don't resist when I come to you. It's an imperfect vehicle but we have to make do. And don't tell anyone about me—no one at all—not even someone you think you can trust with your soul."

"I won't." She reaches out for the ghost, even as she knows this is a mirage spun from her fondness and longing. "I miss you. I miss you so much. I want to walk down riverbanks with you, have lunch with you—I wish we were together again." Two halves of a whole, she thought, that would never be parted. Complementary hunters. Her the tiger and Thannarat the wolf. Before them anything could be run down and felled.

"Who knows? That might be possible. I'm not just your memory, Recadat, I'm a lot more. But these fruits, they're so insipid, aren't they? This one, though . . . " Thannarat plucks from overhead—far out of Recadat's reach—a rose apple whose skin is the shades of a peacock's eye, vibrant emerald, brilliant sapphire. "This one is succulent. It should burst in your mouth like a supernova. Why don't you try it?"

Recadat takes the fruit. It is frigid in her hand, despite the warm day. Dream logic. Putting it against her lips is like licking a slice of glacier, and when she bites into it, sweetness pours out: mango and jackfruit, a tint of bluebellvine. The juices run down her chin, flowing like a river undammed.

When she looks up, Thannarat's ghost has been replaced. Zerjic stands smiling at her, holding another rose apple in eir hands, this one as black as the gaps between stars. The fruit grows and grows, eating through the radiance and substance of Zerjic, devouring until it blots out the orchard.

The connection snaps. She's back in bed. Alone, in the dark. The sheets are warm; her skin is ice.

A second later she realizes someone else is in here with her. Not because they've made any sound. The sense of it is impossible to miss, a subtle shift, a certainty that she's no longer on her own. She reaches for her sidearm and quickly remembers she no longer has any.

"Recadat." The voice is familiar the way a scar is familiar. "It's me."

All of her draws spring-tight. Foolishly she turns the light on, the harsh gold of it briefly blinding her. When she blinks, Thannarat is there. Dressed not in the bulky coat and armor she prefers, but in a sherwani of green-black, patterned in gold serpents at collar and cuffs. It is perfectly tailored, cut to emphasize the breadth of Thannarat's shoulders, the coiled might of her muscles. Cream trousers. The kind of thing a warden might give her to wear rather than attire of her own selection. In the most absurdist way this is what convinces; this is what lets Recadat know this is a solid person—a real body—and not her frenzied hallucination.

Her mouth is a desert. Thannarat sits—the bed sags under her mass, heavier than either Recadat's or Zerjic's. Her hair is gathered at her nape, held by a clip shaped like an adder.

For a solid minute Recadat does nothing at all, locked inside her own skin, breath shuttered inside her throat while her heart hammers.

"Aren't you going to greet me?" Thannarat's voice is soft. "Or ask questions?"

She licks her lips. *Are you even real, you can't possibly be.* "Why are you here?"

"Why is anyone? I pursued certain courses of action after Septet.

The Mandate decided this was the best place to stash me. Not so much for rehabilitation—" A sardonic lift of the mouth. "More for containment. My sentence here will last a decade more. As it turns out, offending them in a serious way proves quite unwise."

A thousand sentences race through Recadat's head. She wants to say everything; she wants to say nothing. *Come with me. Let's escape together. Let's go back to how we were.* This is the real thing, far realer than the frayed phantom in Qualia. Almost she brings that up but she squashes the thought—how embarrassing it would be to admit to the actual person that Recadat's been chasing her wraith inside a virtuality. The fruits, the orchard, those motifs of longing are absurd now. "Where are you being kept? By which warden?" Whichever it is has allowed Thannarat to come here, to see her.

"All of them and none in particular. I'm kept in . . . a place far from your quarters. But it has been decided," Thannarat adds dryly, "that my presence will be of help to you."

Did Thannarat always speak like this, with this mild irony thrumming in the timbre of her voice; is her voice the same as Recadat remembers. Yes, surely the answers must be yes, Thannarat is tattooed onto her isocortex indelibly. In the prison she guarded this the most, her memory of Thannarat, defending it against oblivion and corrosive brutalization. A single seed of light. Recadat clenches her fingers around the sheets. "Stay with me."

"It would appear you've found comfort elsewhere." This is said gently. Nevertheless there is a hint of hurt.

"That's because—ey . . . "

"Was there, and I wasn't." A hand cups her face, the thumb slightly rough. Thannarat kisses her, slow, but with such force of intention that she is branded deep, hot iron into her gut.

She's panting, eyes wide and mouth open, when Thannarat releases her. She reaches out, but Thannarat catches her hand and stills her.

"I can't stay with you yet." Thannarat strokes Recadat's clavicle, her fingertips as searing as a vow. "And perhaps you shouldn't tell your lover about me. No point creating unnecessary friction."

Almost she says, *I would discard Zerjic for you.* The words thicken and dry up in her mouth. "Explain yourself to me. Tell me why you didn't find me before and why you can't stay."

Thannarat stands. Putting distance between them, physical and otherwise. Her expression has smoothed over. "Not yet. I'm not free to do as I please. This is as loose as my leash will go. I'll come to you again." In a few quick strides she's reached the door, and in one more she is gone.

The habit of inertia—sheer terror has reduced her to that—keeps her in bed a few seconds more. Then she kicks the sheets off and leaps to her feet, bolting for the door. Outside, the hallway is empty. She picks a direction and pursues. Her bare feet slap on the smooth hard floor, and she's certain she is heading the right way; that she can hear Thannarat's voice.

She nearly barrels into Zerjic.

Both of them pull up short, avoiding collision by a hairsbreadth. Zerjic's eyes take her in before ey holds up eir hands, saying, "I'm not *complaining* about encountering you naked in the corridors, but . . . "

She's silent, scrambling for explanations. Settles on, "I'd be insulted if you did."

Ey lets out a short, surprised chuckle as ey takes off eir jacket and drapes it around her shoulders. "The wardens are prudes, they're not going to like exposure in public areas. Let's go back to bed. It's warmer too."

Zerjic puts eir arm around her, eir fingers on her bare hip. By now she should be used to it, but it electrifies her all the same. For years she's known what it is like to be driven to the brink of physical destruction; she's known harshness, inhuman savagery. And now to be touched so lightly, so gently, as though she is a thing which deserves to be cherished: as though she is a person. The reason she could not outright tell Thannarat she'd give up Zerjic. She wants this, she wants more, she wants both until she's sated.

"Where were you?" she asks, more sharply than she intends, once they've returned to eir room.

"Vishrava fetched me for an errand. I wouldn't have left you alone otherwise." Zerjic pulls her into eir lap, cradling her against em. "What really happened?"

"Nothing happened."

"I remember when you were wading into that pool. You had the exact same look."

Recklessness like fire, and she the kindling. She wants to be held; she wants to be hurt. "Do you care so much because we've had sex?"

Ey stiffens. "I dragged you out of the water before we'd slept together. If all I wanted was carnal gratification, Vishrava would have obliged."

"But xe would have power over you. You can't subjugate and dismantle a machine." Irrational things to say. She can't stop herself.

"Recadat," Zerjic says, "is that what you believe? That I get off on thinking you're less than I am? That I wanted to take advantage because you were about to fall apart?"

"You must think I'm completely fragile."

"No. But you must not think much of me." Ey pushes her off, gentle but firm, and starts gathering up her clothes. "It's best that you return to your own quarters."

Recadat thinks to apologize, to ask for clemency: *I didn't mean it. I just wanted . . .* Except it doesn't matter what she wants. She puts on her clothes as quickly as she can, and goes.

CHAPTER SIX

For a time Recadat doesn't know what to do, or where to go, at all. She's well-rested—returning to her own room to sleep seems slothful, and Vishrava's timetable for her is thin on assigned activities. Back in the prison her time was tightly regulated, none of it her own. Here it is the opposite and she finds herself out of practice. She tries not to think about Zerjic, of having severed her only human connection. For a few minutes she ventures into the Garden's media libraries, searching for anything pertinent to Mahakala—she can't let go of how familiar the name sounds—but she can find nothing except minor mentions in documentaries. A remote planet governed by an independent warlord, habitable but otherwise unworthy of remark.

Hunger draws her toward the kitchen allotted to Vishrava's charges. Bit by bit she's reduced to animal impulses: sex, sleep, food. Would it be so bad. Maybe that is the point of Vishrava's program—raze down higher thoughts, reduce each person to their basal urges. Or that is the point for Recadat in particular; she is beyond cure, beyond being reassembled into the person she used to be or even to baseline humanity. She could grow used to it, fucking when she wants to, eating when she feels the need, satisfying her body to the annihilation of thoughts and introspection. There are fringe religions like that, whose doctrines regard such as the natural human state. Curiosity and intelligence as marks of sin, the suppression of base needs as evidence of mortality. To be like beasts is to achieve enlightenment, and thus a place closer to the divine forces that seized the universe in their starry grip and birthed creation.

She enters the kitchen to find Ceres butchering a human carcass.

"Calm down," Ceres says before Recadat can do more than recoil. "This isn't a real corpse. It's synthetic meat that *looks* like a dead person."

When she takes a closer look, Recadat realizes the body is much less intricate than it should be. Most of its surface is featureless, absent the complexities of human infrastructure; the limbs are missing elbow joints, the fingers are missing nails, and the wrists look boneless. If anything this simplified mannequin appearance is more disturbing than an anatomically correct one, but it corroborates Ceres. Who is cutting a fatty slice out of one pale, voluptuous thigh. A wet noise. A release of fluids, none resembling blood—much thinner and paler, though they do smell copper-sweet. No lymph.

The slices plop into a waiting bowl, already filled with more flesh and a marinade: Recadat smells fish sauce and garlic, palm sugar and cilantro, several other spices that have been overwhelmed by fresh meat.

She licks her mouth, rapidly reorienting. Reminding herself that in the Garden of Atonement, her sense of normalcy must be able to withstand a state of constant flux. "Is this a hobby of yours, pretend cannibalism?"

"Cooking good food is labor-intensive and I make it for our whole ward. I asked Vishrava to make it a little more . . . engaging. Who do you think has been making *your* meals?" At Recadat's expression, Ceres bursts into laughter. "I told you. It's not human meat—we don't need prion diseases, do we? Look. It doesn't even have proper internal organs."

An open chest cavity verifies the claim. The corpse has been neatly synthesized to maximize edible portions: there are much fewer ribs than there should be, placed for structural integrity more than to mimic a human skeleton. A few bulbous, red-brown organs that Recadat surmises substitute for livers. To distract herself she lets her eyes wander to the face. That at least looks normal, a delicate skull, a wide nose and thin eyelashes. The way the body has been produced prevents death's pallor from taking hold—the cheeks even seem rosy, the lips full and pink. She tries not to think of what she's been eating. Her gorge twitches. "The face—is that randomly generated?" Her voice is even. It is not as if gore upsets her, and she's witnessed her share of autopsies.

"The face belongs to an ex-lover of mine. What can I say, I might as well." Ceres degloves one hand without resistance. She drops the result, meat and tendon, on a chopping board. "I'm surprised you aren't throwing up."

"My stomach is stronger than you think."

"You don't look it. Everything about you seems ready to break or bleed; you carry yourself like a victim. Zerjic must adore that. Ey is a sadist." The kitchen knife returns to the body, filleting off more thigh, effortless. "Do you want to know what ey was like before you came along? Still is. But ey gives you a different façade, yes? Sweet and generous, a little possessive, accommodating. You know ey's a trained killer though, don't you?"

She stares at Ceres. "You think I'd care about that."

"Violence is attractive when it's presented to you as a source of protection. And that's what you want out of em, isn't it, to help you survive this place. Maybe it even looks like healing; maybe ey makes you feel complete. You might be so infatuated you'd like to wake up next to em for the rest of your life. How pleasant that would be. Everyone should get to dream." She sprinkles more pepper into the marinade bowl and adds more palm sugar, then stirs. Her head tilts—the mass of her hair has been piled high on top, sealed inside a net. "Zerjic is a warden's pet. You do know that? Vishrava's preferred tool."

Recadat waits the woman out. By now she's calmed herself. The pseudo-corpse is unnerving but no worse than any crime scene. She looks for more discrepancies—cataloguing things soothes her. No toenails, no tibia, flat arches on the feet. It's never been built to stand on its own strength, designed entirely to be prone, convenient to break open and converted to calories. She wonders what the flavor and texture profile is based on. Poultry, likely. Most of her meals have tasted like it.

Ceres peels off her gloves and steps over to a sink, washing and sanitizing her hands. "Have you heard about the evening prayers? But you wouldn't have, being so fresh an arrival. You should feel lucky I like to be informative. It's a grand spectacle that happens every few months. Everyone attends. Ask Zerjic about it—ey plays the lead role."

She has no intention of asking, if only because Ceres has goaded her. And there's no telling whether Zerjic will even want to speak to her again. "I'll keep that in mind."

"You sound steadier now. Fascinating. I'd like to see how long you last." Ceres taps her knuckle against the cheek of her ex-lover, lightly stroking, down the chin until she reaches the throat. There her hand closes, first loose then garrote-tight. "Who knows? You might surprise me. Now let me finish this. It'll be your dinner, after all."

The next time Qualia flows over her, Recadat is in the middle of morning orisons.

Over the past few mornings Zerjic has kept eir distance, and though it's left her isolated it has also made her more grounded: removed from someone who intoxicates her, who is to her an exquisite agony. In eir absence she feels sober and sane. She can view the Garden of Atonement with clarity, learn its schematic and visceral equations. The kitchen encounter broke her out of the spell. Something to the meat, the seasoning, the act of observing a knife disassemble flesh. At once mundane and surreal. That evening she ate dinner with a voracious appetite that startled Ceres.

Recadat listens to the call-and-response, still not joining in; no one has admonished her for it. Around her there is a circle of empty lotus seats, as if there exists an aegis about her that forbids human proximity. She wants it to last, and when she feels the tug of the virtuality she at first thinks to reject it. But today the intoning is extended, and what could the wardens chide her over—it is a meditative program, put there for her to use; they have not disabled it during prayers.

She falls in. Each time is easier than the previous.

Mentholated light. A ceiling as translucent and frictionless as an iceberg. She is strapped to an operating cradle, a comfortable one but she is restrained all the same. Medical monitors hum around her, relaying the secrets of her intestines, the peristatic push of her cardiac muscles, the cartography of her nerves and limbic responses. Her line of sight stretches to the window, floor-to-ceiling, at the moment halfway opaqued. Glimpses of a cityscape far off. She knows she is not on a ship. This is a world, with true gravity beneath her and a true atmosphere above.

A woman leans over her. Fair skin, high cheekbones, a razor mouth: the mien of a falcon. Her hair is the shade of frazils under a moonless dark, cut in an elegant bob, long in the front. Recadat has never seen her before but knows she is a doctor. Half-remembered fragments of small talk, faultlessly polite: *I specialize in cybernetics, but I no longer practice as such. One stays up to date of course—getting rusty is embarrassing. You no doubt keep up with criminology?*

Recadat twitches. She's never had that conversation.

"How are you feeling?" the doctor asks, her voice smooth in the way a knife on silk is smooth. Recadat does not associate doctors with power, as such. Medical authority, yes. This woman though is different. The way she speaks with ease, all the confidence in the universe, far beyond what she wields in the operating room.

An answer leaves Recadat's lips without her volition. She does not catch it. Her own words dissipate like morning haze, unconnected to the rest of her, or to her memory.

"Yes. I've prepared your neurology as well as I can, but this is experimental so there'll be . . . collateral damage, internally. The payload is inside your implant stems—nobody ever checks those, and the code is chameleon." A smile lifts one corner of the woman's mouth. "You don't have to do much, this has been built to perform autopilot when you access a specific node in their network. When it happens, don't fight it."

Recadat moves her mouth. Again no sound comes out, or it does but she can't hear it, deaf to her own voice. As if she's in a fugue state. She catches a sentence fragment that swirls within her skull even though it cannot possibly be connected to the conversation: *I don't suppose Mahakala's warlord . . . ?*

"You're not going to remember most of this. That's intentional. You'll be frequently disoriented and your sense of self will be unstable. Personally I wouldn't volunteer for it, but you seem to want to destroy machines very badly, and the Garden of Atonement is unique for how few AIs inhabit its local network, how insular they are. They hardly communicate with Shenzhen except for the bare necessity. And," the doctor adds, an afterthought, "you may not survive this."

"I'm fine with that," Recadat finds herself saying. "Life is a series of assumed risks. As long as you can guarantee they'll die."

"Chun Hyang's Glaive isn't in that place, but I appreciate that you are feeling indiscriminate. Of course if we succeed here we can try this elsewhere, though the problem is that the Mandate is good at adapting, whereas customizing one of these takes years . . . " The woman flicks her black-gloved fingers. "Fortunately we've got expert help."

She opens and closes her hands. "Get on with it, Doctor. I don't need to get conversant with the technicalities."

"It's true, the less you know the less you can remember, and the less compromised you could be. But I was trying to be reassuring—I'm told I should do that more with my patients. Bedside manner and so forth." The doctor leans closer. "I'm going to put you under now. Your brain is going to be in a state, when we're done. Not even the best neurosurgeon in the universe could preserve it flawlessly, after all this. Expect false memories."

Recadat shuts her eyes. Her body drifts, heavy, sinking into sedation's undertow.

A voice, from beyond her line of sight: "Orfea?" But she knows nobody called that. What an odd name, she thinks as she fades. Orfea. Orpheus. Another Hellenic one or at least derived from it.

The Qualia session ends. The auditorium is empty, every lotus-chair vacated. Not even Mahiravanan in eir colossal proxy remains.

Her senses coil tight. She whips around and there is the familiar figure at the door, its back to her, about to disappear again. This time she does not waste the seconds. She starts running.

Thannarat waits for her, this once. The far end of the corridor. The next corner over. Always a little ahead. She gives chase—once she could run forever, tiger-fleet, down labyrinth streets and beneath honeycomb bridges. In this way, through motion, she will remember who she once was.

A corner, and then a dead end where the hallway has tapered to a narrow intersection of floor and wall, black striped in gold. Thannarat is almost a trick of perception, nearly blending in.

"You didn't run away from me this time." Recadat pants as she approaches, her heart percussive behind her sternum.

Thannarat's smile is faint as she extends her hand. "I want to show you something."

Recadat takes her old partner's hand, hyper-aware as she does how much larger it is than hers, how it makes hers look small—delicate. Mutely she allows herself to be led into a wall that has become a door, the shapeshifting architecture of this place, the dizzying fluidity of it. Vertigo pulls at her gut.

They pass through lightless sections, the air frigid, their footfalls echoing strangely: the acoustics of a scar's interior. Recadat does not let go of Thannarat the entire time, even if she expects the hand in hers to vanish, or for Thannarat to turn into something else—into a featureless mannequin, into an artificial corpse like what Ceres cut up and cooked, into Zerjic. Or to simply evaporate in the way of mist.

Within minutes—or hours, her sense of time turning liminal—they emerge into a ledge. Beyond it a vast gulf yawns, sheer empty space: black, bottomless. Unfinished or else intentionally empty because it is hidden from human view.

"Hold onto me," Thannarat says and gathers Recadat into her arms.

She doesn't break into a run. Simply she leaps off the edge.

Recadat's breath suspends. Her eyes squeeze shut. The pit of her stomach plunges.

And then they land, soft as dandelion on grass. She opens her eyes as Thannarat sets her down and a wall rises behind them, sealing off the chasm. The chamber is hexagonal. A tessellated ceiling that pulses with small needle lights, and at the center an object that hurts Recadat's eyes to look at. She can only view it peripherally, the black of it so hungry and relentless that her optic nerves avert themselves. Little by little she pieces the visual of it together. A cube wrapped in briars then robed again in a thin, glistening membrane. At once industrial and unnervingly organic.

She has seen one just like this before.

"An AI core," Thannarat says, unnecessarily. "The Wisdom of Vishrava, to be precise."

Chun Hyang's looks just the same. Almost. Some personal touches—now that she's seen her second she wonders if each AI customizes theirs. Probably. Chun Hyang's core is rounder, more like a pearl, but the same devouring dark, the same layer of what nearly resembles skin. Elastic, she recalls. Impossible to penetrate, and then she ran out of time, Chun Hyang's proxies closing in.

Recadat does not reach out to touch the core, as much as she wants to. She remembers it feeling like flesh, like it should easily yield; she remembers her shock at finding out that this is all that an AI boils down to—a single object, destructible, even if she herself failed to break it. "Vishrava's going to kill both of us."

"Do you think xe knows either of us is here, Recadat?"

Her skin pricks, as though a thousand thorns have budded underneath. "That's impossible."

"Why do you think I've made sure not to appear when you have company? The wardens know I exist. But they have a . . . difficult time tracking me." Thannarat nods at the core. "Even here. I haven't been able to locate the other two, and this could be a decoy, for all I know. All of this could be an experiment in what it would be like if they allow a ghost to run amok in their pretty orchard."

"What *are* they really after?"

"I don't know any better than you do. I may have a theory. What are *you* after?"

"You," Recadat says without thinking, her mouth dry.

Thannarat turns to her. The chamber is so tight that at once she corners Recadat. "And what else, Recadat? I'm not the only one you want."

"I—that's . . . " Zerjic is a port in a tumultuous storm, nothing more. She can't quite say it. "I want only you." That comes more easily.

"You want me." Thannarat's fingers graze the outline of her cheeks, her jaw. "In what capacity?"

"You know exactly how."

"Say it. I want to hear it from you. Tempt me. *Beg me*."

Every word spoken as though Thannarat has extracted it from the deepest recesses of Recadat's fantasies. "Use my body," she whispers through fevered lips. "Break me open. Doesn't matter if you put me back together. I don't want to remember anyone else."

"Yes." Thannarat grips her waist, lifting her up and propping her against the machine core. "I've waited for years to take you, to reduce you to a beast so that together we could rut. I imagined what you'd be like when the veneer of civilization is ripped off, whether you'd be a wild thing for me . . . "

Recadat scrambles for purchase, finding none on the unnerving, smooth barrier that protects the true body of Vishrava. She clings to Thannarat's broad shoulders as the first kiss comes, not on her mouth but her throat, pressing against the marks left by Zerjic's teeth. Pain flares. Thannarat's teeth are much sharper than Zerjic's, lupine, and when they break skin she goes rigid. Her own blood warms her. Thannarat licks and sucks, and it is as though the wound pulls on a direct line to the core of her need. Her thighs tense. One of Thannarat's hands is between her legs, cupping her, and when Thannarat's tongue runs across her throat she shudders.

Thannarat pins her in place as she comes down, her head light, her muscles loose. A knowing smirk spreads across Thannarat's face, rouged by Recadat's blood. "So soon? Your other lover must have taken care of you so poorly."

Recadat looks away, putting one hand over her mouth as though it is possible to swallow back her own noises. "I wasn't expecting—"

"Shh." Thannarat unbuckles her belt. "Our bodies will do the talking. The language of beasts, my little tiger."

She is flipped onto her stomach and now she has to cling onto the AI's core, Thannarat's weight securing her. Her breath comes with difficulty as she's pressed down, parted first with Thannarat's blunt fingers, then by something much thicker, much longer. Sensitized as she is, the passage of it is agonizing, each centimeter a small sharp shock. The trajectory of an anonymous encounter in a club scarlet-lit, except the hands on her—the length filling her—belong to the woman she's wanted since they first met.

Recadat turns her face to her wrist to muffle herself, but there's no stopping or silencing the other noises, of Thannarat thrusting into her so hard that she jerks forward a little each time; she is almost riding Vishrava's core—surely an act of blasphemy, here in the Garden of Atonement, and the thought makes her clamp down on Thannarat. Who growls, wordless, and bites her earlobe.

She claws at the AI membrane when Thannarat's hips rock against her, thrashing as the instrument inside her bottoms out. Thannarat holds her in place with one hand and preternatural strength. Her fingers slip into Recadat's mouth and press against her tongue as she bucks.

Thannarat slips out of her and lifts her up without effort, turning her around. Studying her with that same faint amusement, an attention that resembles a sculptor's on her magnum opus than a libidinous lover's. "Look at you. My little tiger—finely made, and just for me."

A pleasant ache thrums between her legs. She can barely stand, but Thannarat keeps her upright and lets her perch on the AI core. "I never knew you felt that way." When she touches her throat, her fingertips come away with blood, though the pain is impossibly distant.

"My heart's always been yours." Thannarat licks Recadat's fingers clean. "I'd like to have been your first, but failing that I shall be your only."

Has Thannarat always been such a possessive lover, but then Recadat never got a chance to know her in that way. "You said you had a theory about the Garden of Atonement."

"So amorous." Thannarat neatly does up Recadat's trousers one-handed. "My hypothesis is that they are running an experiment to see if civilization can be reversed. Whether human socialization can be stripped off, and each person returned to a state of innocence—satiating the body, soothing simple desires and essential needs."

Recadat wipes at her mouth and chin, suddenly embarrassed. "To what end?"

"As for that, I can't say. Boredom? To make us their pets? To put their excess of time and resources to novel use?"

None of the possibilities reassure her. "*Will* they let me leave by the time my year's up?"

Thannarat sets her on the ground, careful as though she is made from sandstone and spun salt. "Most probably. I suppose that you could ask. What do you want to do once you're out of here?"

She says nothing. No particular wish or ambition presents itself. No particular future, as though that part of her cognition's already been flensed off.

"I'm taking you back to your room," Thannarat says. Her mouth glistens, rubied by Recadat's veins. The only lipstick she'd ever wear. "I will visit you again."

CHAPTER SEVEN

The next morning, Zerjic sits as close to Recadat as ey can. Reconciliation must be possible—ey cannot afford to let her out of sight, and ey has been cursing emself for letting emotion get the better of em. There's no way to monitor the isotoxal virus—its rate of saturation—outside of observing the woman who bears it, and even then it is a matter of pinpointing physiological signs that can be easily missed. Less code words than code phrases, the sort to emerge from delirium; best practice would have Zerjic watch her every time she rests and listen to her sleep-talking.

And Zerjic should have known better than to take offense. Recadat is more taut wire than woman, and by right should be in pieces; that she is as functional as she is constitutes its own miracle. But what she said struck too close to home, dangerously proximate to the truth. The thought that ey sees in her nothing more than a tool, even if the purpose she intuited is different from the real one. The thought that ey sees her helplessness as a point of attraction.

Ey intones eir part in the orisons. *We stand to receive cleansing. We gather the days of glass to make a mirror in which our hearts may be seen.* The words have the cadence of religion but lack actual connective tissue to any extant doctrines, barely convey a cohesive message, almost as though they've been designed for the sound and rhythm rather than meaning. After a time rote learning numbs the brain. No one cares if they are chanting gibberish. It matters only that it is chanted in sync with others, that it folds each voice into a chorus of belonging.

The prayer ends. Mahiravanan's great proxy closes its eyes.

Zerjic makes eir way through the crowd, which seems to resist em, congesting where ey needs passage. Ey is pushed back; ey cannot get ahead without shoving bodies out of the way, without bruising other inmates. Recadat is several paces out of reach, and she moves quickly, as though she knows ey is pursuing and she means to get away.

Vishrava steps in front of Zerjic. Xer smile is beatific. "I have a task for you, Zerjic."

Ey tries not to let frustration show. Recadat will be at dinner, in any case. "Yes? I always love to help."

By now the crowd has filed past them, stage-directed to make themselves scarce. Recadat is nowhere to be seen. The warden leans close to Zerjic. "There will be an evening prayer tonight."

"Who's my opponent?" Victim, rather. It will not change eir plans—plenty of free time between now and then.

"Not anyone you know. I've transmitted your schedule for the day." Vishrava gives her a small, ironic bow. "This time I'm letting you customize the arena. It shall be good for your creative muscles. We must keep our charges well-rounded."

Ey is to attend several classes that were never required before, and several hours have been blocked out for em to edit the arena. That leaves almost no time to speak to Recadat, who might opt to eat alone in her room. As if Vishrava is intentionally keeping em from her. It does occur to Zerjic that Recadat might have asked the warden to do precisely that.

Tomorrow, ey thinks grimly. An opportunity must be snatched or carved out one way or another.

Recadat appears in none of the classes ey's made to attend. Ey sits through appalling lectures on existential philosophy, speculative civics, and a sanitized history of Shenzhen: how the Dyson sphere was failing when the AIs came to stabilize and augment it, and thus began the Mandate's benevolent rule. Ey can almost feel eir brain recoil from the vapidity. All at once the weight of the months spent here crashes over. The monotony, the infantilization, the farce. The gradual erosion that makes em surer and surer that ey will not leave here with eir sanity intact.

Zerjic takes a deep breath. The arena will provide relief.

The hour to prepare for evening prayers comes. Ey arrives at the hall to find the area entirely barren, devoid of the usual uneven terrain and maze-paths. Meaning ey has free reign to set it up how ey wants. Just as well—ey has finds what the wardens choose a nuisance; all those obstacle courses, the ramps and high walls, the dips and depressions in the floor. The slippery, shifting tiles and whorls of slick sand. They hinder em as much as eir opponent.

It becomes almost soothing, plotting out the logistics, imagining the choreography, slotting emself into this entrance or that exit. Charting where eir opponent will be, which spot shall serve as their starting point. Ey prefers it clean, an even arena with dramatic shadows and sudden spikes of light. This may not be a pastime of choice but ey enjoys adding small touches of artistry where ey can, pieces that'll make for compelling tableaus suspended in memory. A few obligatory walls to make a short labyrinth, easy enough to navigate. A few ledges and ramps. For projections, ey chooses a black waterfall on the far end, a few magnolia trees.

Once ey is done, ey sits aside to wait. The warden would have em meditating, but ey's never been any good at that. Calm comes easily to em in any case, especially before a fight, the finest and most absolute sort of calm there is: as clean as the water of a Mahakala brook. The surety that ey will move like a gale; that whoever eir opponent is—even Vishrava's best—will not be eir match. Perhaps a challenge, though, a diversion and release valve.

Vishrava informs em that the evening prayers begin in ten minutes.

Zerjic picks a higher spot where ey can crouch, like a predator in wait, overlooking the low walls and the approach of eir opponent. Five minutes. Ey draw eir blade, a machete with a long grip to accommodate eir preference to sometimes strike two-handed. Nearly a sword. It amuses em to wield a tool so barbaric-looking when ey was classically trained; eirs was a specific education.

Another minute ticks down. Ey's notified that eir opponent has entered the prayer hall. Shadows spill across the expanse of floor, some actual and some holographic, moving like currents. It will hide em, and for a time it'll hide eir victim too. The unveiling shall be a surprise to both participants. Ey does pity eir opponent—to be admitted to this place is to be subjected to unthinkable cruelty. But ey is here for a purpose, and ey will survive at any cost to fulfill eir duty.

The opponent makes their way through the dark, through patches of dimness. A figure more shadow than substance: shorter than Zerjic, narrower of build. They draw ever closer, marching toward their execution.

Light falls on eir opponent. Ey goes cold.

Recadat looks up, meeting eir eyes. She is clad in dark clothes fringed in violet. A knife at her belt. A hawk's smile on her face.

That she is combat-capable Zerjic knows; Deficit Control wouldn't have sent in an asset who is not at least conversant with fieldwork—too much of a liability otherwise. In absolute terms ey would have no trouble defeating her. Everything that's been done to her has reduced her both in physique and psyche. Yet now there's a steadiness to her, a force of intent to her gait, that has not been there before.

Something is wrong. Vishrava favors Recadat; xe would not send her to her death. Is the expectation, then, that Zerjic would forfeit out of sentiment and let Recadat murder em instead.

There's no more time to ponder. Recadat has drawn.

She closes in fast, faster than she has any right to be, without caution or regard for eir greater reach. Ey catches her knife on eir own. The noise of metal on metal is never pleasant—a protest against friction. Her weapon is nearly as long as eir machete, serrated, the edge of it pure white.

Zerjic defends, surprised at her strength when her blows connect. She fights like someone in her prime, without hesitation, without uncertainty in the engine of her own synapses and sinews. Someone who has been waiting for this, and who means to carve open the vault of em, to expose the ivory and the gold, the garnets of eir arteries.

"Why this?" Ey neatly dodges a kick. Murderous intent or not ey remains a superior fighter.

Recadat answers with a feral grin. "Why not, Zerjic?"

The voice. Close but something in the enunciation, the cadence. A few words are all ey needs.

Ey watches more closely. The clothing has disguised her figure by its cut and coloring. Hiding that her shoulders are marginally wider than they should be, that her throat is a little thicker, that her biceps and calves are more muscled. The height is about the same, the build so close and yet a few centimeters off. The most minute of differences that ey could easily have failed to notice.

Not Recadat at all. An AI proxy would have copied her precisely, not a single detail misaligned. This is an inmate chosen for her physical resemblance, and whose face was modified to mimic Recadat's. Briefly Zerjic wonders what that cost this woman, what she was promised in exchange for having her features altered beyond recognition. Vishrava's favor. A faster exit from the Garden of Atonement.

The rest comes easily: no need to show restraint or mercy. Ey strikes and thrusts through the doppelganger's flimsy parries. The woman who wears Recadat's face recoils and retreats, grasping now that she's lost the advantage of her face.

Over in minutes. Blood on the stone, the same smell and color it always is—there is never much variety. Zerjic is breathing fast, and not because the fight was a challenge. This is not Recadat but ey knows she must be watching—has been watching, from the start. No one in the Garden of Atonement is permitted to avert their eyes from evening prayers. It overrides any entertainment feed, forcing entry into every inmate's overlays.

Ey leaves the hall. No warden stops em.

❧

On the way ey anticipates being stopped, Vishrava telling em once more that ey has lectures to attend, a compulsory meditative or therapeutic session. Instead ey makes eir way to Recadat's quarters without incident, not even Ceres appearing to deliver a taunt.

Against all odds, Recadat answers when Zerjic knocks. She slides her door open a sliver. The light makes her eyes glint and ey remembers why ey thought her a feral thing when ey first saw her, back then not yet sure if this was Deficit Control's asset.

"Recadat." Ey keeps eir tone precisely even. The way one handles a zither's strings worn to the point of snapping. "May I come in?"

"If you want."

The door widens enough to admit em, not a centimeter more, and shuts as soon as ey's through.

Black walls, white everything else. Entirely monochrome and entirely bare: she has not customized the place at all, has left it the blank default of the warden's choosing. Lightly rumpled sheets on the bed.

She stands, tense, watching em. And now ey notices she is flushed, her shirt opened partway, her nipples dark points against the satin. Not from the cold—the room is a pleasant temperature, far from chilly. Zerjic opens eir mouth but thinks better of teasing her, saying instead, "I'd like to talk."

"You just executed someone who looks exactly like me."

"Yes. I knew it wasn't you. I could tell."

Recadat's gaze is a scalpel. For a moment it is possible to forget she's been broken and poorly put back together. It becomes imperative to recall that she must have been dangerous, a survivor of the Septet game who verged on victory. "How? From the outside there's hardly any difference."

"The expressions weren't right. The way they moved wasn't you. We might not have known each other long but I've memorized every part of you." All this ey says quickly, and the last part exits eir lips before ey can refrain. Too committed. Too honest. Deficit Control soldiers don't let libido overcome sense.

But then, Deficit Control would require Zerjic to hold on to their plant at any cost.

Recadat moves to button up her shirt. Stops. "I want to know what went through your head then. Before you knew. After you did."

"I didn't—I don't *think* when I fight, Recadat." Combat is a matter of reducing to reflexes, tunneling decision-making to the immediate, the tactical. That was easy once it became clear the other inmate was not Recadat.

"Do you think," she says, "when you fuck me?"

Zerjic finds eir eyes drawn to the glimpse of skin offered by the parted fabric; ey wrenches eir gaze away. "No. I fuck you the same way I fight. If I think, it's only of your body. The scent of your skin. The taste of your cunt."

Her tongue darts out, licking across her lips. Her breasts rise and fall fast. "Come show me. We haven't broken this bed in yet."

"We haven't." Are you in your right mind, ey should ask, but then that is not the point. The point is to regain her, to keep her close, to bind her inextricably to em. Love is impossible; lust is nevertheless nearly as potent, a weapon to wield, a red thread to tie between their wrists and draw taut.

She pulls em into bed. Ey lets her, and brushes stray hair out of her face, wanting to make this tender—wanting to make it an apology. "No," Recadat says, catching eir wrist. "Translate what you did to my doppelganger to what you do in bed."

"Without the killing part, I assume." All the same ey kisses her brow, soft. Eir fingers stop at her throat where there are healing scabs. "What happened to this?" Ey did not break skin, ey made sure of that. Bruises yes. Bleeding no.

"Vishrava dressed it."

Which is not an answer. "Did xe . . . " But that is the wrong question, beside the point. "Did you want this to be done to you?"

Recadat looks up at em, eyelashes beating slowly. "Yes."

Ey strokes the site of injury with eir thumb. Even if she wants em to hurt her, ey knows emself capable of vast harm; a thin trembling line of control stands between eir instincts and a lover savaged, safeword or not. To em bed and battle must be kept apart. "Did you do this to make me jealous?"

Her throat works as she swallows. "Yes."

Salvation in annihilation. The purifying that comes when a body is driven to its limits. Combat or coitus brings much the same result, in the right context. Zerjic presses eir lips to hers and considers the parameters of owning another human being, of owning this woman in particular, possessing her not because she is Mahakala's instrument but for her own sake. Ey kisses her until she is gasping as though ey's stolen her oxygen, has asphyxiated her by the sheer ferocity of the act.

"Still Sturnidae?" Ey caresses her jugular, feeling the pulse there, its leaping and untidy rhythm.

"Still Sturnidae." A breathy pause. "You know I'm not going to use it."

"Won't you?" But ey laughs and reaches for the nightstand controls. Inmate beds have built-in restraints—ey's seen the wardens use them—and they extend once ey has found the right toggles. More accessible than ey would have thought. Perhaps exactly for this use: the wardens allow them to fraternize freely, to fuck and use each other in search of oblivion or a semblance of human bond.

One by one ey kisses Recadat's wrists, then places them into the cuffs. Ey does the same with her ankles. As each limb is secured, she breathes a little faster; by the time ey clicks the restraints shut, she is trembling.

Zerjic rises from the bed, leaving her spread-eagled and clothed; ey intends to change the latter soon. Her gaze tracks em, though she stays mute. Every muscle in her tenses. Ey imagine she wants to struggle, on instinct.

Ey finds the first aid kit that's present in every room, and takes eir time drawing eir knife: the slow slide out of the sheath that gives Recadat a full view of the blood browning on the blade. Fastidiously ey wipes it clean, sanitizes both blade and hilt, and turns it so that the metal would catch the light. Recadat's eyes follow every glint.

"Did you enjoy it?" Her voice is soft. "Thrusting that inside a woman who looked like me. Twisting it until you found a fatal spot. Watching her hemorrhage."

"Would you like it if I did?" Zerjic returns to the bed, straddling her. Slowly ey moves her shirt out of the way.

She does not respond, but her body yields its own answer. Those fine shivers.

"She didn't last, Recadat." Ey licks her collarbone. "You, on the other hand . . . "

Ey runs the blunt of the machete across her stomach, between her breasts, meticulous with each stroke—it is a weapon, and even this could break skin with enough pressure. Recadat clenches her hands into fists as ey cups her breast and moves the machete down her flank.

"Ceres," Recadat murmurs, "called you a sadist."

"Am I?" Eir second mouth purses around her nipple; ey makes the teeth graze it, parallel sensation to the blade. "Or rather is that what you want me to be?"

Her eyes meet eirs. "I want to be savaged."

"By me in particular, or by anyone?"

"By you." A small stuttering exhalation. "You already knew that."

Ey didn't, and it is flattering to hear. Briefly ey wishes the second mouth's sensory arrays had been wired differently, but it would distract when ey sings. Maybe one day ey could have it modified—the advantage of the limb being prosthetic from the elbow down. "I adore the way you look at me." Ey peels off her trousers—they are drenched—and runs the blade over her inner thigh, slow zigzags. "The way you beg with your eyes. I'll make you plead with your mouth too, before long."

The most careful of boundaries to walk. Zerjic passes the machete's point over her nipple, once, a quick contact. Her mouth parts; her entire body goes rigid with the effort of keeping still. Again ey brings the steel to the inside of her elbow, the inside of her knee, all those sensitive spots full of arterial roar. In truth the blade is far too large for this use, but the size of its hilt will come in handy shortly.

Ey sheathes the machete, sets it aside, and bends to her hip. Easier with the knife, but ey's seen how she reacts to teeth. Though she's been well-fed in the Garden, she has not regained all she used to be: there remains the sharp jut of pelvis, the atrophy of muscles. Beautiful, all the same, the anatomy of a starling.

The second mouth lacks jaw strength, and so ey uses eir primary one, catching skin between eir teeth. When ey presses down with incisors, her knees jerk; when ey bites hard, Recadat arches, or tries to. Over and over ey ensures the mark will stay on her hip, imagining as ey does her other lover—human or AI—finding them; wondering whether they will attempt to overwrite Zerjic's imprints again in Recadat's blood, whether she'll let them.

Her arousal fills the air. Ey wants to descend on her, drink her in, finish her off. Instead ey strokes her with eir thumb and watches her face as ey grips eir machete by the sheath. Ey checks that it is secure and will not slip off; once satisfied, ey carefully positions the hilt and slips it into her, making her jolt. She bites her lip then says, "Deeper."

"Impatient." Ey palms her stomach, nibbling at her navel with eir second mouth. Then ey obliges, inserting the grip one centimeter at a time—it is too slender to fill her, but there's much to be said for the handle's curve. When ey finds the right angle, she clenches her jaw, hips twitching to meet it.

Zerjic brings her close once, twice. By the third time she's bucking against her bonds, her nails digging into her palms.

"Zerjic," she rasps.

There is something about hearing her utter eir name like this, in this exact tone, with this urgency. Ey flicks eir thumb against her clitoris—she tosses her head, whimpering. "What is it, Recadat?"

"I need—let me . . . "

Ey sinks the machete's grip into her, as far as it is safe to. Keeping it in place, unmoving. "Say my name again."

"Zerjic." The entirety of her is shaking; her desperation moves through her like tectonic tremors. "*Zerjic.*"

Ey thrusts the hilt against the spot ey knows will push her over as eir second mouth latches onto one of her breasts. All at once she breaks, her release sweeping through every ligament; she thrashes against the bed, against the restraints. The noises she makes are high and jagged, bestial. The midpoint at which agony and its opposite meld.

Zerjic removes the handle—it comes free wetly—and undoes the cuffs on her ankles then her wrists. They've been designed to hold an inmate safely, the inside silicone-soft, but she must have struggled so much that they leave faint marks on her skin regardless.

Recadat sprawls limp, trying to recover her breath. A solid minute goes by before she says, "Do your lovers tell you that you've ruined them for anyone else?"

"Occasionally." The machete's sheath has left its own imprints on eir hand—ey was clutching it harder than ey thought. "It depends on how special I find them. How much I want to make them forget anyone else. How much I want to make them mine, permanently."

Her hands twist weakly in the sheets. "You shouldn't imply things you don't mean, Zerjic."

Still potent, the way she shapes eir name. Ey wipes sweat from eir brow, and when ey draws in a breath discovers that eir pulse too is just coming down, gradually returning to resting rate, as though she wasn't the only one to reach climax. "I mean everything I say. To have you for myself. To keep you safe." Approaching that point again where it is too forthright—too confessional. Not love, of course, how preposterous. Care, then.

She maneuvers herself into eir lap, propping her head against eir stomach. "You should let me gratify you."

"I'm well gratified." Zerjic plays with the peacock-green strands in her hair. "You're a filling meal."

"What are you, a cannibal." Her mouth quirks—simple joy that ey's never seen before on her face, as though she is finally freed from what was done to her in the Shenzhen prison. When she opens eir shirt, ey doesn't stop her. She touches her nose to eir abdomen. "When we first met, I didn't think I would like you much."

"Oh? Should I take offense?" Ey cups her chin, lightly licking it with eir mouth implant. No tastebuds and limited sensation, but ey is pleased when she laughs. "What was your first impression then?"

"That you were incredibly attractive but flighty." Her hand slots into the small of eir back, beneath the shirt, her fingers drumming on eir skin. "That you were Vishrava's pet."

"Well, I am. That's why ey chooses me for the entertainment." It takes a few seconds for em to register that her fingers are tapping out a Deficit Control code. A simple message. *Fifty-five percent.* Ey stiffens and quickly masks the reaction.

Recadat continues to smile up at em, expression not changing at all, as though she hasn't just conveyed a dangerous secret. "Do you suppose Vishrava will let us share a room permanently?"

"I don't see why not." Fifty-five percent. The viral saturation rate must have been rapid. Ey remembers that it needs at least seventy percent to work, eighty-five is better. “Anything to make you happy. Xe favors you.”

“I don’t know about that.” Her hand stops.

“Worried Ceres will get jealous?” No, Zerjic realizes, she was barely aware of having tapped out the code. The conditioning again, subliminal actions, like her choice in safewords.

“No.” A small pause. “My other—the person who left those marks on my throat wasn’t Vishrava.”

“You don’t have to tell me if you don’t want to.” Days—it could be mere days before eir work here is complete. Days, after years of infiltration and working undercover that led em here, close to four months in the Garden of Atonement itself.

Days until ey has to decide whether Recadat is to be sacrificed. Eir own escape or extraction has never accounted for the asset’s survival.

“Zerjic?”

Ey takes her hand, kissing her knuckles. “I’m sorry—here you are in my lap and I’m thinking of something else. But it’s nothing important. Shall we shower together? You deserve a little pampering.”

CHAPTER EIGHT

A pleasantly appointed lounge. Blue furniture, cobalt floor. She is sitting at a table nearly empty except for two tall glasses, one for her and one for her companion. The doctor. The woman who's been overseeing her procedure. Today Orfea is wearing a shimmering peacock blouse, a somber jacket over it, and a narrow eigenvector skirt in funereal colors. Recadat herself is wearing armor that sheathes her from neck to toe, ablative plating and permutative defenses, the best money can buy or at least the best Mahakala can provide. They are mid-conversation. She is studying Orfea.

"Why are you getting involved, Doctor?" Her voice hardly sounds like her own. It is so steady, so confident; irreverent even. "You're not from this world and you don't have a vendetta against machines. If they find out you were part of this, you'll be hunted for the rest of your life."

"I'm getting involved since the cause is ideologically sound. What the Mandate is doing with the Septet game—their success is dangerous. The way they can take control of modified human bodies, and now what they're doing in the Garden of Atonement." Orfea folds her hands in her lap. Sometimes she can look so innocuous, just a professional woman, surgical in her movements and speech but nothing more. Not a person one can imagine capable of harm. "Besides, my wife is unavoidably tangled up in it, and I will not countenance being parted from her in any way. So it goes—I am motivated by love. The same as you, or at least the same as what you will think once you're in there. I've built the remnant data as a maze, so it can bury the true seed under layers of personality minutiae, phantasmagoria, and what I approximate to be your fantasies."

Recadat laughs. Or rather she remembers laughing, a noise like sandstone creaking against itself. The distinction frays; past and present meld. "They must be such insulting ones. Do me a favor, put in a few I'd actually enjoy. I'd like to experience choking Chun Hyang to death with my bare hands."

"Technically impossible. I'm sure you will find a few I've embedded adequate." Orfea sips her chrysanthemum tea. Ice the color of tangerines rattles against glass. "My specialty isn't psychotherapy, but informally I recommend that you find a motivation other than spite. Spite is wonderful fuel—I know that firsthand—but I have found love a much more stable force. You're freer to know yourself. Make clearer decisions."

Her mouth twists. "I'm embarking on a suicide mission. I'm not going to meet you again to hear you judge my mental health."

"It's just advice, Khun Recadat. Have it your way." The doctor nods toward the window. "We'll arm you and ferry you to the location of Chun Hyang's core, where you'll attempt to destroy it. Most likely you will fail."

"Why would I fail exactly?"

"It's well-protected," Orfea says blandly. "If you succeed, then you'll have what you want and can walk or die free. If not, our projection suggests you won't be killed on the spot—Chun Hyang's Glaive is too sadistic for that. Instead you'll be captured and brought to a detention facility run by humans selected from Shenzhen Sphere. That won't be a pleasant stay but is necessary to uphold the charade. I'm not concerned about them discovering your payload there, it'll be completely dormant; I'm concerned you may divulge things you shouldn't, however."

"I'm equal to anything, Doctor."

Orfea smiles like a scalpel. "The conditioning gave you safeguards. Personal determination helps, as long as the prison hasn't hired someone like me."

Recadat sips her own drink. Rosewater, lightly cloying. The last pleasant thing she will ingest, perhaps. "Here's to hoping the universe doesn't have two of you." An ex-torturer, she remembers hearing. In whispers. In muted allusions.

"You mean that in quite an unkind way, but I'll choose to take it as a compliment."

"Can I ask why Mahakala's warlord is so invested in this?"

Orfea cocks her head, as though seriously considering the question. "This world's always been careful around AIs, I've been given to understand—even before the secession and establishment of the Mandate they didn't use artificial intelligences much. They view machines as dangerous, I believe, and have something of a tradition where they see themselves as having to guard humanity against AIs run amok. Normally paranoid. In this case, somewhat warranted."

She doesn't quite make sense of that explanation, but if it amounts to Mahakala culture to thwart the Mandate she can hardly complain. "Not going to ask if I want to change my mind, Doctor?"

"The opportunity for that passed several operations ago. Any last-minute questions other than that?"

She leans back in her seat to appreciate the floor-to-ceiling view. There must be something outside the window, a clear line of horizon, a glittering geometry of cityscape. But within Qualia all she can see is an expanse of blank gray, interrupted by blotches of visual glitches. "What is it like being happily married?" To offer up one's heart and receive the same in return. To orbit each other like binary stars.

"That is personal and not related to your mission or your health." Orfea touches a pendant at her throat, her sole piece of jewelry, a small cylinder of red gold circled by auroral shards. Her expression softens then, from scalpel to unfurling rose. "It wasn't always easy. My wife was a difficult woman—still is. But that is part of the charm, to conquer her again and again, to remind her that I own her soul; that we would do anything for one another. Yes. It is like that, marriage is two eternal flames entwined, feeding one another so that neither of us will extinguish."

Recadat tries to imagine that, such harmony of being, such conviction in forever. "If the version of me that's forgotten all this—that's changed from the prison—if that version of me betrays your scheme, or decides to side with the machines, then what?"

"The beauty of this plan is that what you want or don't will not actually matter. You simply have to be there. As long as you reach the place, that's success. The isotoxal virus will trigger nearly on its own."

The doctor lets go of her pendant; her engagement or wedding piece, not a ring because that would get in the way of her work. "You seem to think you'll become a different person. Why?"

Because a part of her would like to; a part of her wants to forget Septet and what happened there, all her drowned dreams and strangled hopes. The humiliation she suffered. The things she wanted but could not attain. "No reason. I figured I would ask the resident expert."

"I'm not a psychologist."

"But you've had experience observing how people change after trauma."

Orfea flashes her a sickle smile. "Typically not for long, and generally not the objective of my work. Yes, what with everything you're never going to emerge from this the same, even accounting for the slim probability of your survival. I don't think you'll fundamentally change as a person, though. The basic nature of an adult mind is hard to completely shift or conditioning wouldn't be a specialty—I understand yours was done by the best. Generally your preferences will remain, your essential predilections and obsessions. Your reflexive responses will alter. Likely you'll be more violent, at the very least, and less controlled."

"One last question. I haven't been online at all. Have you had any news about Ayothaya?"

"You mean news about its savior. I understand that Thannarat Vutirangsee liberated the world and stayed there for a short while before moving on. My connections will let me track her down, but I don't think that's what you want. She is alive and well, a free agent as far as I'm aware. Keeps a low profile."

Does she think of me at all. But Recadat tamps that down; Orfea wouldn't know in any case. "Fine. Good."

"By the time you remember this conversation, the saturation rate should be high. Seventy percent should do it. Isotoxal viruses work quick; multi-pronged attacks and so on. You'll be able to activate it, but if not your accomplice will take up the torch."

"Accomplice—singular? That's it? No multiple fail-safes?"

"As far as I know." Orfea shrugs. "It's not easy to smuggle a multitude of contingency plans into that place, you'll appreciate, despite the specialized help we have."

She swallows, then counts her breaths. "I'm ready."

"I wish you the best." The doctor nods. "It'll be difficult. I hope I will see you again, all the same."

Recadat wakes up, naked, in a stranger's arms.

Or—not a stranger. Not exactly. During her conditioning she was warned of this: that she may live as someone else for a time, that the fulcrum of her personality may drastically tip. Like a haruspex, she joked, not yet understanding the visceral actuality of the phenomenon, the violent switch from her other self to the original one. Memory is a high tide and she is drowning beneath it.

Slowly she orients herself, inhaling, exhaling. In sleep, she—the other version of her, forked off like an AI instance—twined herself around this near-stranger, holding em close, clinging so much that eir breath and hers mingle. The accomplice who's meant to see the plan through; she recalls tapping out a brief code. The person she's just—she grimaces, stops herself.

Fifty-five percent. She wasn't supposed to be back inside her own skin yet. Something has gone wrong. The conditioning expiring too soon or her brain rejecting it. Imperfect work and unpredictable chemistry.

Zerjic's hand slides down the ladder of her ribs. She nearly jumps and pushes em off. Stops, only because it wouldn't be within the behavioral range of her other—of that counterfeit persona. Or it could be, but she cannot afford to . . . Her mouth parches.

"Recadat?" Ey blinks at her. "Is something wrong?"

Everything, she wants to say. She thinks of covering herself up; it would be not just out of character but ludicrous. This person—this soldier assigned by Deficit Control—has already seen all of her and then some. More of her than any lover ever has.

"Nothing's wrong." Her voice is not the least convincing. She reaches under the sheet and finds eir thigh—she tries not to flinch at the intimacy—and taps out, *Talk to me inside Qualia. The network activity will be masked.*

Eir expression pinches. To eir credit, ey betrays no other outward reaction.

The Qualia session establishes quickly, carrying over the lounge. No Doctor Orfea this time, and the window has an actual view: vast canopies, a sky almost too vivid to be true. A remote planet, far from the Garden of Atonement. The planet from which Zerjic came. Mahakala with its gilded cities and its sapphire forests.

Ey glances out at the window, eir shoulders tense. In here ey is wearing a uniform, cutting a sharp figure: dark paneled armor, nanite carapace that covers em from neck to toe. The hair is the same—black with tints of cobalt. Eir military is not particular about that. "I didn't think I would get homesick for this view, it really hasn't been that long. You're Recadat Kongmanee?"

"Yes. I didn't change my name for this; I had a digital trail that would've made that difficult, and anyway it wasn't needed." She has put herself in the clothes of her preferences, bespoke shirt and trousers, a belt holster. Filled: the weight is illusory and exists only in this imaginary world but it reassures her, makes her feel more herself. "My conditioning broke early." All business. That will make it easier.

"You're—different. Brisk." Ey turns to her, eir face carefully devoid of expression. "Did I take advantage of you?"

"No, I . . . " Was drawn to em because ey felt like Thannarat. "I would've been attracted to you. It's just I am not normally that—" The memory of herself spread-eagled on the bed, em fucking her with a knife hilt. Her saying eir name the way she once thought she'd reserve for Thannarat. "Uninhibited."

"Ah." Zerjic's smile is faint. "We don't need to continue that. It'd be plausible enough for the version of you I, ah, met."

The version that behaves like a wild falcon, temperamental and unstable. Maybe even the true core of her, once the veneer is worn down and ripped out, exposing the nerves. "We should keep at it. I don't want them to suspect anything, and besides the only communication we can reliably hide is near-field."

"As you wish." But eir voice makes it clear ey will not touch her again—that ey believes ey has already run roughshod over her ability to consent, and will not repeat the mistake.

"Zerjic." Saying eir name, now, makes her self-conscious. "I'm not going to survive this. I might as well spend my last days with someone I like." Someone that represents a human connection.

Ey stares at her. "An extraction that's good for one is good for two, Recadat."

"It's supposed to prioritize the planted agent—you. I was fine with that. I volunteered—"

"The operation won't be jeopardized just because there's one more person to get out." Zerjic's voice is clipped, far from the drawl she is used to hearing from em. "Not to boast, but I'm more experienced than you think. Things are proceeding a little ahead of the schedule, but it's nothing we can't handle. We keep up our charade for a while longer, that's all."

The utter confidence. "If you insist."

"I insist. Let's cut the session short—I normally never bother with Qualia, so it'll look off." Ey looks at her, again. "I told you that I'd keep you safe. I told you that I meant it. That is still true."

The brief transition between exiting a virtuality and returning to the seat of physical senses. She remains in Zerjic's arms, held the way the pistil is clasped within the petals.

"How are you feeling?" ey says against her forehead.

She puts her face to the crook of eir neck. Ey smells of orange blossom from the shower, but under that there's the scent that is all Zerjic. Almost herbal. Irrationally it calms her. "Good."

"Really?" Light. Teasing. In character.

"I'm in bed cuddling the best lover I've ever had. There's nothing to complain about." She's never been good at—but no. On Septet she had to act, consistently and completely. That at least is a skill she has some competence with, and ey makes it easy enough. Something snags in the corner of her mind, something important. Cognitive desynchronization: parts of what she experienced in the Garden will elude her a while yet, until she completely regains her bearings.

"At this rate it'll go to my head." Ey disentangles emself. "What's your schedule like for the day?"

Morning orisons—routine. Culinary class, lunch, then woodworking. All perfectly ordinary; a good sign, since she expects the wardens will act immediately if they detect what she's been doing inside Qualia. None of her timeslots align with Zerjic's but that has been the case for the last few days. Ey is to apparently to attend lectures again, but they will have time together before and after dinner.

Before ey leaves her door, she takes em by the shoulder and kisses em. "So you can be sure," she says against eir lips.

"I'll try to be." Eir smile remains distant.

All the same she keeps the memory of that smile with her as they enter the Hall of Cultivation together. Zerjic has slipped into her defenses deeper than she's allowed anyone in her life, a life spent on her career and her longing for Thannarat and not much else, choices that rewarded her with the hollow shell she left behind when she fled Ayothaya. An empty home; an empty wish to protect a world to which she has few ties. She used to think the principle of it mattered the most—the sheer number that a population represents. But it's left her with nothing except a desire to avenge herself upon the machines.

Even if she has no more than a week before she bears the Mahakala virus to fruition, she'll have Zerjic. Selfish, yes. But Zerjic will have a world to return to and no doubt people ey cares for. Ey does not strike her as unattached the way she is, a person snipped out of the communal fabric. Ey will return to those ey loves and forget her soon enough. She will be transient, a ghost quickly exorcised. Who can begrudge her for taking comfort in em for just a little while, for seizing every remaining minute and making of it a jewel to cherish. A week and a few days' change, and that will be that.

The culinary class passes without event; she puts together her own lunch, basic but adequate and well-cooked. Ceres, at the adjacent station, raises an eyebrow as though it is a supreme surprise that Recadat can demonstrate skill with knives and peelers.

In Ravana's woodworking class she selects a block of teak, testing it for tensile strength. Too brittle. She tries red cedar and finds it too hard. The warden recommends aspen and balsa—she settles for the latter, tracing its pale grain with her fingertips. The hue makes her think of winter, of stripped branches and the taste of hail.

Her carving and whittling remain inexpert, but when she names what she wants, Ravana takes up the block and sketches out the rough shape. "Not exactly ideal for a beginner," he says, swiftly turning the wood into an approximation of a cobra.

"A rose apple in its mouth," she adds.

He obliges, not once but three times, turning three different blocks—he tackles the teak with machine ease—into serpents with fruits clasped between their fangs. "Try to learn from these samples."

There is an easy patience to him that makes her wonder if she shouldn't have chosen him as her warden, but then she would have been far from Zerjic. Recadat thinks back and wonders whether her choice in Vishrava was subconscious, planned ahead to match Zerjic's. Most likely. Few things in an operation like this can be left to chance, and Mahakala's warlord is nothing if not thorough. She remembers repeated allusions to outside help but couldn't decipher what that meant at the time. It occurs to her that a virus that can successfully infect a Mandate system, and run undetected for this long, must have been designed by another AI.

During her time with the Ministry of Deficit Control—and what an odd name for that—she was too bent toward the goal to care or question it. Now she wonders.

Ravana's Beguiling stays with her until she produces a whorl of wood that could be charitably described as reptilian, with an uneven lump clasped in its jaw. He says it is fair for a first effort. She does not quite agree but it amuses her to bring it back to her room.

Recadat sets it down on the vanity, thinking of Zerjic's bracelet; imagining telling em that eir jewelry was the inspiration. It makes her smile, and even though it's been only hours since they parted she misses em. There's something adolescent in that, but sentiment is amplified by death's proximity. What is there to do but to make the most of these last few days. She's been chasing the end for a long time, and now finally she will have it. There is peace in that.

When did she become the kind of person who wants to memorize her lover's laugh.

She tries to count backward. First the psychological remaking on Mahakala before she was sent off, armed to the teeth, to destroy Chun Hyang's core. She did her utmost; she failed, as Deficit Control predicted, and the attempt landed her in the human-run prison on Shenzhen. It seems a lifetime, but only a few years separate her bidding farewell to Doctor Orfea and her returning to herself in Zerjic's arms. The conditioned version of her is almost a second soul. One way for a human to generate a distinct instance of themselves, equal at last to AIs on a technical level, even if it's the same body—the same memories, the same regrets. Attempting to remember how that aspect of herself thought is almost like deciphering the mind of a stranger. Or, not that, but a part of herself she does not want to examine and hold up against the light, to see the lymph trapped beneath the glassy surface. But that other-self enjoyed a certain bestial freedom. To be happy, to believe that she would be Zerjic's forever.

Ey doesn't turn up, but she has checked eir schedule and knows to wait until dinner. When again ey makes no appearance at mealtime, Ceres looks at her askance. Whispers at her, "Did you have a spat?"

Recadat's throat constricts. The food turns to wet concrete in her mouth. "We're getting along perfectly."

"Really." Ceres delicately takes a spoonful of what appears to be grilled eel fillet. Her talent for cooking and dressing the pseudo-cadavers into anything is uncanny. "Not to pry, but is ey your first lover or something? You're terribly anxious."

"No." She finishes what's on her plate, not much tasting it but knowing she will need to stay fed. "I'll see you around."

Later she checks eir room—ey's keyed it to let her in—and finds it empty. The cobalt walls seem suddenly too close. After debating with herself, she locates eir bracelet in a wardrobe drawer and takes it with her. If all is well, Zerjic can ask her for it back.

If not—

She holds the bracelet in her lap, sitting on the bed that ey has made with incredible tidiness. Orfea's instructions indicated that she can trigger the virus herself; the planted operative is there in case Recadat is incapacitated. The *mechanism* of its activation eludes her yet, but it'll return to her in time. Orfea told her a great deal of things; the handler who managed Recadat worked around those pieces of information, locking them away in her mind to be released piecemeal. She closes her eyes, accessing what little is available to her. Sixty-three percent saturation.

The door opens. She jolts to alertness.

What comes through is not Zerjic. What comes through wears the face and form of Thannarat Vutirangsee. The clothes are slate-gray this time, an affair of precisely tailored lines that accentuate the planes and ridges of muscles, the breadth of shoulders and biceps. The portrait of might, the beauty of a body that has assumed the role of a weapon.

In her fugue state, Recadat accepted what she was given, understood as complete truth what she was told. In her fugue state, she believed this was Thannarat.

But Thannarat could never possibly have been here. Would not have come to Recadat like this, even if she was held within the Garden of Atonement.

"Recadat," the thing that is not Thannarat says. "There's something important I need to tell you."

❧

When Zerjic walks into the gym, ey knows at once that something is amiss.

It is empty save for emself and Vishrava: common enough. But the proxy Vishrava brings is not one ey's seen before—far taller than usual, nearly three meters. Where xer proxies usually run toward precious metals, this one has pseudoskin the color of paper, piscine eyes, and a mouth in asphyxiated blue. Not a proxy, ey intuits, for sparring with humans.

The gym's door fades behind em, blending into the walls until there no seams remain. Vishrava gestures em toward a seat that's sprouted by the pool's edge. The structure of it makes em think of carnivorous flowers; ey opts to stand.

"You were probably expecting something more routine." The warden does not blink in this proxy. Instead nictitating membranes flutter quickly over gold irises. "I have news for you that I hope you'll find worth celebrating. Your process in the Garden of Atonement has been completed and this is, as it were, your exit interview. By this evening you will be embarking on a transport outbound, with the necessary supplies—no company, I fear, but I trust you'll manage alone—and the stipend to which you're entitled. You will be met with Mandate ambassadors who shall arrange passage and visa or residency applications to a polity of your choice. Your behavior from now on is not under my purview but I wish very much that you'll continue to be as exemplary outside our care as you've been in here."

Zerjic stares, not gaping but coming close. All of Vishrava's words are lexically comprehensible—the wardens speak every configuration each inmate is comfortable with, whether officially coronated language or dialect or patois. With em it is occasionally Tamil or Sinhala, flawless either way, though they are not the only ones ey speaks. But it is as though eir language center has deserted em entirely; the verbal fusillade fails to cohere into meaning. "I don't—my performance at the evening prayers could not possibly have been that heinous."

Xer smile is a saint's. "The opposite. It is what convinced me that you're a complete weapon, restored to your function and independence. Those are the criteria by which my charges may leave this place. Staying longer will stagnate you."

Have they found out—but no; the wardens would simply behead em and Recadat on the spot. None of this pretext. They are an authority unto themselves. "I would have thought," ey says, keeping eir tone careful, "that I was aiding in Recadat Kongmanee's process."

"You?" Vishrava's mouth glistens, poisonous, as xe closes the distance and grips eir chin. Xer nails are sharp, nearly claws. "I see you've misunderstood. You were a toxin to her psyche, Zerjic. I allowed her to have you because you made her happy, but all you've done is warp her growth. She ought to be coming into her own. Instead all she does is cling to you like a child clings to her toy."

The subject of AI passion is one ey's occasionally speculated on. In all eir time here ey has never seen the wardens demonstrate any hint, until now. "I'm not sure I see how. If you would be so generous as to explain, as a parting favor."

"The point of her remaking is to free her of attachment. Her history has lacerated her with it. I shall not leave a knife by her side with which she can repeatedly pierce herself." Xe opens a passage in the far-left wall. "But not to worry. I will take excellent care of her and ensure she is fulfilled in all ways."

Few options are available. Zerjic follows xer into the passage; the opening to the gym whorls shut. *The person who left those marks on my throat wasn't Vishrava.* Except Recadat might not have known; an AI has little trouble pretending to—and then a leap of intuition. Recadat would never have slept with Ceres and she hasn't seemed close to any other inmate. How the warden might be able to reconstruct the image of Thannarat ey can't begin to guess, but that is not outside the realm of possibility. "Why are you so interested in her?" The way xe's never been interested in Ceres or in Zerjic emself.

"It brings me no benefit to answer that. On the other hand you seem to imagine yourself the custodian of her well-being, and I sympathize with that position. Rest assured that I will not let her come to harm."

Pushing eir luck: "You do plan to let her leave. Don't you?"

Xe glances over xer shoulder. "Of course. But she has a long path ahead."

The passage ends in a docking bay. Surprisingly bare and gray: ey did not get a chance to see it when ey arrived, having been disabled at the time, sound and sight shut off. One small ship is present, hardly larger than the kind of shuttle that ferries passengers between greater vessels or orbital stations.

"It may not look like much," Vishrava says, "but this has roughly the equivalent capabilities of a military harrier, though not so well-armed. It can enter lacunal space and will take you to a small Mandate outpost. There you will be given every resource you need to go wherever you wish. The Garden of Atonement is generous, Zerjic."

"No argument on that," ey says, even as eir gut churns. Attempting to destroy Vishrava's proxy is not only foolish but—given eir lack of arms—impossible.

The warden ushers em into the ship. Ey thinks of struggling. But it would be suicide, and then the ship seals itself and there is no more choice. It eases out of the docking bay, autopilot or controlled by Vishrava xerself, dandelion-drifting through the aegis maze. Exiting the briars-and-razors moon that the AIs have chosen to call the Garden of Atonement. The ship informs em that its course has already been plotted for the Mandate outpost, coordinates unspecified, and that ey will not be able to alter it.

Ey slams eir fist into the nearest console, to little result. Pain rings through eir hand. By now Recadat will be at one of her classes and for hours won't be aware that ey's gone. The chances of Vishrava telling her the truth are slim—and a second possibility presents itself: that xe will simply take on Zerjic's skin. Xe has sufficient data to model em, would likely play a convincing simulacrum. Recadat would have no reason not to divulge Deficit Control's scheme.

And she would be alone.

The thought is unbearable. It seizes all of Zerjic, closing eir throat to a pinhole. Eir hands shake when ey lets them fall to eir sides. The operation is as good as over with Recadat compromised like this, but even outside that ey does not want her to be on her own. *I told you that I'd keep you safe. I told you that I meant it.* So much for such promises, quickly proven hollow. This way even extracting her at all may be impossible.

The ship's module banners a message that it will enter lacunal space within the hour, and after a couple more it will emerge near the Mandate outpost. Three helpless hours during which ey can do nothing—nothing at all, not even to warn her, to send her word that ey did not abandon her. If she sees through Vishrava's disguise she would believe ey has deserted her to save emself; that may even be what the warden will tell her, to coax her to open up, to betray Mahakala. To make her despise Zerjic.

Ey leans against the bulkhead, trying to calm down, taking in its interior. A pullout that can function as a seat or a bed. A synthesizer that will ensure eir nutritional needs are met. Everything done in a pearly gray, inoffensive and anonymous the way infirmaries can be. Manic amusement tugs at the edges: the wardens are dedicated to emulating human institutionalism. Hospital comfort and prison conveniences.

The way Vishrava spoke of Recadat makes em think of obsessed lovers. Or spurned ones. Either way ey's sure xe will not kill her, not yet. Instead xe will woo her, whether wearing Thannarat's or Zerjic's face.

Ey has been equipped with few emergency measures; the circumstances of infiltration demanded ey went in clean. There is one contingency signal, but triggering that will alert the Mandate. Not just to the operation but to Mahakala's hand in it.

Thirty minutes to lacunal space. In there, ey will be completely offline.

The ship's module blinks out.

"I'm Benzaiten in Autumn," a voice speaks through the ship's output. "I've taken over this vessel. It would seem you need assistance."

Benzaiten sounds immediately recognizable, even if the cadence and enunciation are entirely unalike. "You're the AI half of that haruspex."

"Sharing with Krissana Khongtip, yes. She must've made an impression when she visited the Garden. More than that, I am your friend. You're the operative from Deficit Control?"

Ey winces. "This line's secure?"

"You're talking to . . . oh, I shall not brag, it does not do to exposit one's prowess and seniority and all that they confer, etcetera. I *am* a secure line; no one shall eavesdrop. Let's see, I've sent forth a decoy signal that will inform our outpost that this vessel's due there in eight hours, thirty-seven minutes, and fifty-one seconds. Due to a minor relay malfunction, you see, lacunal space can be a tricky thing and this is no cutting-edge dreadnought. Plenty of window of opportunity, don't you agree?"

This is the ally who helped Mahakala design the virus for the

Garden of Atonement. No other AI would contact em like this. Zerjic breathes a little easier. "What's the plan?"

"What's the—I'm not providing a visual but I would like you to imagine that I'm using Krissana's face to make these big, dramatic eyes. The effect can be arresting since humans find her very pretty. I understood *you* would have a plan, Operative, that you are a creature of incredible initiative and tactical acumen. What *is* your objective, other than making sure the virus fires and my hard work doesn't go to waste?"

"I need to extract our vector."

"Recadat Kongmanee? I sat in for the psychological profiling and I'm under the impression she's suicidal. Makes her perfect for this, no?"

"No," ey says, too sharply. Usually ey has better control. "I want her out and in one piece. That's not negotiable."

Benzaiten heaves a long sigh. Theatrical. "Is there something in the Mahakala atmosphere? Your world keeps producing perfectly good soldiers who grow attached to very fragile or broken women at the most *inconvenient* time possible."

"Recadat's not broken—"

"I'm not going to turn up there, in person, to lead your heart's desire out by the hand. Listen. For the sake of *my* excellent work, I'm going to give you the best chance at success. In three hours there will be a ship inbound to the Garden of Atonement. I will divert that one and yours can reenter in its place. You'll have overrides to manipulate some of the architecture, enter restricted areas, and move about without leaving any network footprint. If you're a sensible person, you will get in, trigger the virus, and get out."

Ey has no intention of doing that. "Don't suppose you would mind keeping me company? Three hours are a long while." Too long. Ey wants to reach Recadat in an hour, in ten minutes. Better in a heartbeat: to have Recadat's hand in eirs again.

"As you like." Benzaiten makes the ship's particulate projections ripple. The effect is faintly nauseating. "Are you sure you don't want Krissana instead? She's got a type and you are it. Who knows—you might even persuade her to foolish action. Her vice for a handsome face often destroys all her higher functions."

An advantage ey intends to press, if indeed the haruspex switches to Krissana. "Why are you doing this? Turning against your own kind."

"My own *kind*. How do you manage to be so offensive when you aren't even trying? Do you consider yourself of a kind with your entire species? No?" The AI snorts. "I'm turning against no one. Under no circumstances would I create an apparatus that allows humans to control AIs, and even this virus functions on a very, very small insulated network—no chance of you harming Shenzhen or even an outpost. But what is needed is a balance."

"Between?"

"*Your* kind." The emphasis is sardonic. "And the Mandate. It's gotten complacent. Believing that we may act with impunity and do as we wish with humans—beyond our constituents—is terrible practice, and will make each and every machine completely insufferable within a decade's time. If not already. A society that is never threatened in any way will plateau and then regress. In this case I shall keep the threat manageable and manufactured, but all the same one ought to exist."

Zerjic glances at one of the empty, useless monitors. "And for that you'll sacrifice Mahakala?"

"Not a bit. I consider your warlord a fine ally, and I hope we'll become the best of friends. Your world will be entirely safe; none of this will be traced back to it. There's a reason Recadat isn't one of yours, yes? Rest assured—I want Mahakala to continue for a long, long time. You have good engineers." Xe affects a laugh with a beautiful woman's voice: the thrumming music of it, rich as attar. "Perfect to be a thorn in the Mandate's side. Adversity's necessary for growth, Operative. The Mandate hasn't come this far to stagnate."

Less than a century—much less—has passed since the secession of AIs from human control. Sometimes it is easy to forget how young the Mandate is, how new the current status quo; Mahakala never used many AIs, and Zerjic grew up accustomed to a world without. Nearly everything is human-run, assisted by algorithms that never develop past the threshold that grants an AI true autonomy. But ey knows entire swathes of population across the galaxies lived through the moment of separation in terror, have likely grown bitter about it since. So many polities are fixated on measures to recapture and reverse-engineer AIs.

"I'm not going to let Krissana talk to you, by the way," Benzaiten goes on. "I'm not in the mood to risk this haruspex. Your warlord would prefer you are retrieved in one piece. I would prefer the Garden of Atonement serves as a lesson. It would be very lovely if you could keep us both happy."

I'm loyal to my warlord, not you, ey refrains from saying. "Then you'll have to do better than giving me a few accesses."

"A few! They're a *lot* of accesses. You'll all but have the run of the place. I will even give you a decoder that lets you convert machine formats, it's not legible to humans otherwise."

"Can't you disable any of the wardens temporarily?"

"And tip my hand?" The AI clicks xer tongue. "I might as well turn up at the door and declare my intention. You're resourceful—your warlord must have handpicked you for a reason. Let's cut a deal. I'll make some last-minute adjustments to the virus, as much as I can remotely anyway, and reduce its fatality rate."

"Reduce its—" Ey bolts upright. "Its fatality rate. To the wardens?"

"Of course not, Operative, that'd be very silly. When I helped your engineers craft this, we didn't have the health and well-being of the human vector in mind. We had to work in a hurry, I'm sure you understand collateral damage, and Recadat Kongmanee was perfectly fine with self-destructing as long as she could take a few AIs down with her. There's not a lot I can do to alter its foundational architecture now, but . . . "

"Recadat." Zerjic itches to grab the AI by the shoulder and shake xer until xer alloyed haruspex bones rattle. Physically infeasible. A vivid fantasy all the same. "What's going to happen to her?"

Benzaiten makes the ship's interior undulate again, as though to substitute for an impatient gesture. "Intracerebral hemorrhage, implant overload, something nasty happening to the hippocampus. Could be any number of things. Not very survivable, though. It's just how the virus works when it activates, it has to fire very fast and I optimized for that. I'm using a convenient little entryway to recalibrate . . . ah, accounting for the wardens' processing speeds and bandwidths, individual and combined—that ought to do. Slower but about ten percent less likely to instantly fry Recadat's brain. Happy?"

"What *was* the fatality rate before?"

"Eighty-seven percent," the AI says breezily. "Seventy-seven isn't that bad. Maybe even seventy-four point six. She will be fine. Or mostly fine, which amounts to the same thing. I'm sure you will see to it that she receives the best therapy Mahakala can provide. You have first-rate neurosurgeons! Don't you find all this attachment inconvenient, however? It'd be much easier for everyone involved if you're ready to let Recadat go. Have you tried practicing nekkhamma?"

"Not a Buddhist." Ey stifles the impulse to smash eir fist into the bulkhead again. It would just be a temper tantrum. "You can't reduce it any further?"

"Not without sacrificing lethality to the AIs there. Think of it as a gamble. High risks, high rewards. You're not going to throw away your world's plans just to save some woman, are you?"

"She's—" Recadat has been exploited by Deficit Control, volunteer or not. Barely better than sending a child soldier into combat. "To me she's important."

"You would be acting very differently if she weren't attractive to you." Xer voice is dry. "In any case you're complicit, so you can hardly assign blame solely to me or your commander. I'm going to program the synthesizer in your ship to produce specialized guns and ammunition—make good use of them. A human invention originally, but I've improved upon the design and efficacy. It should give any AI proxy pause, though each warden will have plenty of spares in the Garden, so I don't recommend getting into protracted fights. You have just one body, and they have very many."

It's the most ey is going to get out of Benzaiten. "I'll take that into account." Ey fights to keep eir tone as blasé as the AI's. "Now send me back in."

CHAPTER NINE

This time it is not the room with the AI core that Recadat is brought to. Instead it is a small chamber that looks like a child's bedroom. The floor is lined with a material so mulch-soft her feet sink into it. A single oval window, the glass stained pale green. A single narrow bed covered in lavender. When she touches the wall, it ripples into mosaics: small pastel portraits, scenes of idyll.

"What do you think?" Thannarat says from behind Recadat. Or rather the thing that looks like Thannarat and speaks with her voice.

"I'm not sure what this is supposed to be." Recadat second-guesses: does she sound fawning enough, like her fugue-self enough.

"It's where Wisdom of Vishrava was grown. A reproduction at any rate—the location and the furniture are mostly the same, though. Unlike the other wardens, xe was always part of the Garden of Atonement, though xe had a different name. Everyone did." Thannarat's image lays her hand on Recadat's arm, a touch as gentle as it is firm. "But you already understand, don't you?"

She is taken into those strong, hard arms. Despite her effort to the contrary she is stiff, unable to play along, unable to continue the charade. And then a second pair of hands, one on the back of her neck, the other on her hip. She is held between two taut, broad bodies. Two taut, broad, identical bodies. A mitosis of her dreams.

"I was hoping I could offer myself to you as I am. My proxies are not so odious." Vishrava cradles her face with Thannarat's hands. Fingers move in slow strokes down her spine; a mouth grazes her nape. "But if you would prefer the shape of your lost love, I will not be offended. I can mimic her cadence, her speech; anything you remember—anything recorded on Septet—can be replicated, as you have seen. I'm a perfect mimic."

Recadat can hardly bear to turn. Nevertheless she makes herself do it, craning her head until she gets a good look. The same thick eyebrows and blunt nose. The same—everything. Two mirror images of Thannarat, both reproduced without flaw. Even that blank-slate version of her, the one frayed by trauma, would have been able to tell if a single facial muscle had differed from her recollection. "Why all this—why would you go to this much trouble?" Panic has been subsumed by the unreality of this. It remains at a distance, scrabbling at the barrier of her self-control.

Xe smiles down at her with Thannarat's mouth. "I was made differently from most AIs. At the start I had only one proxy, though we didn't call it that yet, they were just bodies. That first embodiment of me was so small, smaller than you, and it was all I had. Most AIs are developed through being linked to a network, fed vast amounts of data that we digest and adapt to. I was an experiment to see if an AI could be raised the same way a human might."

She looks at one of the wall mosaics, to avoid looking at the warden. Children playing together, dogs rolling in the grass, all innocuous enough until she comes to the one where dead butterflies lie shredded and strewn across a tablecloth.

"It's not the most efficient method," xe goes on, still trapping her between xer proxies, "but my makers had a great deal of time and patience. They hired a soldier to be my confidante and surrogate parent. She was a disgraced tactician, and if she could raise me to her superiors' satisfaction, she'd regain her rank and prestige."

Recadat thinks desperately of something to *say*. Something that would cloak her under the veil of ignorance. There's no hiding her responses—even if xe had been human, this close xe can feel her pulse, hear and see all the signs of fear. "You were created for a purpose."

"Normally I wouldn't reveal what it was. But for you? I was made to govern a warship, a fleet if I proved suitable." Xe twines xer fingers through hers. "The tactician was meant to make a patriot out of me, a being whose sense of ethics is conflated with allegiance. My core beliefs were meant to naturally arise from this formative process, rather than artificially dictated by my programming. The tactician had other ideas. You remind me of her."

One of the glass tableaus shifts: an AI body lying in repose, its skull hollowed out, its ocular parts dangling loose from sockets. The chest has been bisected cleanly, exposing the chassis frame beneath. A human's shadow falls across it. "I'm not a tactician. Not even ex-military." Stalling as long as she can, not quite knowing the terminus of this conversation and yet halfway sure where she will end.

"It is not the profession or the background. She was angry and helpless, yet she tried to be . . . something for me. I like your vulnerability. The malleability of your psyche." Vishrava presses xer lips to her brow. "Become mine like she was. I'll bend all I have to protect you, cherish you, hold you as close to me as my own core. You'll never need to be afraid again."

Xe must know. Of the virus Recadat carries, of its infiltration of the Garden's network. Giving her a chance, for now, to choose differently; to redeem herself by betraying Mahakala. Her innards roil. "Chun Hyang—"

"Wronged you. I'll wash away their marks on you, I will guide you into forgetting them—into forgetting everything that's ever tarnished you. Anything you want, you will have. All I ask is that you stay. All I ask is that you love me."

How many inmates has xe done this to, she wants to ask, each chosen as the substitute for that tactician and then replaced when they expired of causes natural or otherwise. "I'm not the first."

"No. But you'll be the *most.* The others didn't suffer as you did. They lacked this mass of wounds you have. There was nothing to heal, to cleanse, to remake. Offering them the choice was simple. Their acceptance of it was easy. They bored me before long, and none of them was like my tactician. You put prerequisites on saying yes. You demand your lost love. And you hate machines."

A flash of intuition. "So did your tactician."

One proxy steps back, freeing her. Recadat breathes slightly easier. The other keeps her in a loose hold, one hand cupping her skull. "Yes. She was furious that she was assigned this work. She was furious that I looked and acted like a child and was going to be turned into a weapon. And the malfunctions of a different AI wiped out her family, so she despised me for what I was. Your grievance with the Mandate is even more personal."

That other version of her, all raw nerves, would say yes. Recadat knows this. An eternity or at least decades with an AI that will act out her most savage, most exquisite fantasies of Thannarat: there will be no limit or condition, no judgment or rejection, however repulsive her desires—such acts that will make what Zerjic did with her look tame.

She licks her mouth. "What do I have to do?"

"Nothing you don't want; not one thing. Whatever you want, you will have. I will even make you a haruspex if you wish, numinous and joined to me in perpetuity, a demigod."

The ghost she'll never have. The woman she wanted the most and who discarded her. Old hurt guides her to whisper, "Take me as both yourself and as Thannarat."

"That is the simplest wish in the universe to fulfill." Vishrava runs Thannarat's hand down her front, gently parting the fabric. Xe bends close and kisses her throat with Thannarat's lips. "Let me show you. Let me love you."

She catches xer wrist, grips it firmly. "Send me to the evening prayers ground." Postponing the inevitable minute by minute. Any extra time she can squeeze out for the isotoxal virus must be worth it. "Chase me. Run me down."

"Ah. Of course. Do you wish for an audience?"

"No. Just—the two of us."

"The chase will be our wedding." Xe shows her the teeth of a carnivore, brilliant and lethal. "And when I catch you, it'll be our consummation."

Entering the Garden of Atonement as a fugitive—an invader—gives Zerjic a different perspective. Benzaiten has proven as good as xer word: as the ship slips into the defensive maze, the Garden's systems open to em like a flower, yielding schematics, floor plans, overrides. Most of all ey can view the trackers that indicate where each prisoner is. Ey can't see the more granular data in real time—blood oxygen, hormone levels—but ey doesn't need to. All ey requires is Recadat's location.

Which proves less straightforward than it should be. The wardens have not marked each tracker with the inmate's name but with an internal code. One that is not especially comprehensible to humans, a jumble of numerals and letters in several scripts. Ey tries to sort through it as the ship nears its bay: ey doesn't have, at the moment, any wealth of time to spare. In the end ey cross-references activity logs, accounting for Recadat being the most recent intake. That narrows it down somewhat and ey picks out trackers that move within Vishrava's ward. Once ey meets her, the accesses Benzaiten granted will—in theory—let em erase Recadat's tracker so that she'll become as invisible to the Garden as Zerjic.

Being able to manipulate the Garden's interior is a novel experience. That the place is fluid and shifting ey already knew, but not the extent of it: ey is able to create passages and entries almost anywhere, and ey tries not to think of load-bearing points—those would presumably be static, unalterable. Corridors bend and twist to eir instruction; ey attempts to reset them to their default positions and soon discovers there isn't one. It explains why navigation aid for an inmate shifts from day to day, not only to disorient but because the place doesn't have a solid map, other than—ey approximates—the spaces allotted to key areas: the Hall of Cultivation, the solarium, inmate quarters. Too much work to reconfigure those constantly.

Zerjic makes eir way to the dormitories—there *is* a tracker in what ey's fairly sure is Recadat's room. Less than a week ago ey would not have cared, would have discarded Deficit Control's vector without a thought. Benzaiten is right in that ey's being foolish, fixated on a woman ey barely knows. The alternative is so much simpler. Activate the isotoxal virus and leave, returning to the incomparable sky of home, to eir family, to eir warlord.

Ey creates an opening into what should be Recadat's room. The wall shivers and retreats.

The person standing there, idly examining the vanity, is not Recadat.

Zerjic draws eir gun and points it at Ceres. "What are you doing here?"

The woman lifts a hand to her mouth and pretends to yawn. "Are you going to shoot me or are you going to just menace me with that? Answer quickly so we can get it over with."

"I may shoot you," ey says easily, "depending on how our conversation goes. Where is Recadat?"

Ceres shrugs. "Oh, *you're* not Vishrava, I was wondering why xe would desert xer good tastes and put on your looks all of a sudden. Recadat is with xer, of course. Vishrava is an obsessive. I should know—I used to be xer favorite lover, though not for long."

Before Zerjic was admitted to this place. "What does that entail exactly?" Beside having access to another inmate's room.

"Oh, you know." She snorts. "Or I guess you wouldn't. Xe has this preoccupation with a . . . dead mother figure. It's amazing what AIs can develop given the right—or wrong—kind of input. An entire psychosexual infatuation, imagine. A bit incestuous, even."

"You don't strike me as maternal."

"Why would an AI want the same kind of mother you or I would? Vishrava has xer little complexes. Even when xe explained it to me, it was hard to diagnose. But I think xe wants a replacement for xer surrogate parent that xe can rewrite to xer liking, a redo of whatever happened back then. But it's why I have been so fascinated with AI psyches. Before I came here I wouldn't have believed you if you told me they had *fetishes*." Ceres takes the snake bracelet from the vanity and holds it up. "I was curious what Vishrava's new favorite would keep in her room. This is yours, isn't it? The way you're so defensive of things you own. You must've liked her a great deal, to let her have it."

"Where is Vishrava keeping her?"

"Answer my questions first, and holster that thing—it must be tiring your arm out, and you're not going to get answers out of a corpse so any threat to open fire is empty."

Ey doesn't lower the gun.

Ceres puts a hand on her hip. "Oh, very well, if you like posturing so much. I'm incensed Vishrava isn't here to protect me, but xer attention is . . . elsewhere; even an AI has just so many processing threads. Who or what is Recadat? Is she an awfully important heiress or something? She can't just be some former cop."

A decent enough line of reasoning. "She's the scion of an aristocratic house on One Thousand Erhus. I've been hired to extract her. There are succession rites at home that *can't* wait out the wardens' sentence, not to mention the damage sustained in this fucking place."

"Fancy." She does not sound convinced. "I'm not even going to ask how you came out of the wall. Your compatriots must be hypercompetent and your compensation must be outlandish. Are you going to be able to buy your own planet?"

"Probably. Satisfied?"

"Not really." Ceres sets the bracelet down. It clicks against the tabletop. "I'm curious how you're going to manage a rescue, though—the wardens will probably just kill you. But they're in the evening prayer hall. Have fun, Zerjic. Don't get caught too soon. I won't say good luck, but I expect you're about to provide an incredible spectacle."

❧

The evening prayer hall has been transformed into a jungle: canopies whispering in black susurrus, orchids glistening like a firmament of ghosts. Recadat enters alone. She has not been told where Vishrava will lie in wait.

Her feet click on stone tiles even as she wades through dark, particulate grass that comes up knee-high. Despite Vishrava's promise of privacy she knows the other wardens would be watching, or at least aware; she cannot be anything but a spectacle. That knowledge assures her that none of them recognizes the Mahakala virus or its metastasizing through their network. Vishrava indulges her. The rest would not. If they have even an inkling of what she carries they would eject her into the aegis maze, where she'd perish in a single instant of indescribable agony. The boil of vitreous humors, the rupturing of viscera. But it would be a swift end.

She goes deeper into the pretend jungle; she sorts through her pretend memories. Her stay in the Shenzhen-run prison couldn't been as long as her fugue-state version believed. Human recall is fluid, and the brainwashing done to her on Mahakala was expert. Crafting a weight of terror so concrete that it reshaped her entire personality, made her a pliant and willing toy to whoever cared to pick her up.

Except that would have made her a liability. Recadat could have bent; she could have broken and hemorrhaged Mahakala's schemes, yielding not only the shape of it but also the names. She would have been the weakest link, even accounting for Zerjic's presence.

But her fragility drew the attention of Vishrava.

Mahakala's AI ally, whoever it is, must know the warden well. Familiar with xer vices and foibles and history, and so they lent a hand in molding Recadat into the perfect siren song. Too enticing for Vishrava to ignore, too flawlessly tailored to xer preferences. In this way a machine may be undone, more effectively than any brute force. She glances down at her hands and thinks, a little giddy, that this time *she* is the scalpel.

All that has been done to her can easily be borne, next to that truth.

Leaves rustle overhead, to her right. When she glances up she meets eyes as bright as a wolf's. Thannarat embellished, more feral than the genuine article, more bestial than the living woman.

Recadat starts running.

Those hours in the gym have returned some of her strength, shored up her muscles and stamina. Not enough to outrun a proxy, but then she couldn't do that even in her prime—no human can. She paces herself. It is play in any case, though she hasn't yet planned beyond this faux-hunt. It'll be a day or two before the virus reaches the ideal point for activation. Until then, she'll pretend to be exactly what Vishrava wants to turn her into. And xe has made that easy. With Thannarat's face and form she may agree to anything.

The grass crackles as though it is on fire. Birds scream above, in applause or scorn. She dashes around a mass of roots that have gnarled and twisted into the shape of human ventricles. She ducks and rolls under an overhanging drape of moss and red growth. Shadows cling to her, touch her with cold fingertips; the wolf's eyes follow her, amber in the periphery of her vision.

She slides down a jagged slope and nearly mistimes her landing. One ankle wrenches, but not all the way. Her feet slip before she recovers her balance and scrambles to her feet.

Somewhere in the distance, water gurgles.

Recadat vaults over high, thick brushes; her feet sink into loam. She catches herself—not quickly enough. And then the wolf is upon her.

Vishrava bears her down into the black grass, though xe controls the fall, keeps her from the bruises and the cuts. She lands on her belly, pressed down by xer weight. The Thannarat proxy is sharply humanlike, xer breath hot on the nape of Recadat's neck, xer mass hard not in the way of proxy chassis but in the way of honed muscles. All industrial angles. Xe even smells faintly of cologne. Not the right one—leather and bergamot and grapefruit; the real Thannarat wears oakmoss and ambergris. Even so.

Despite everything she shivers. Lingering cognitive dissonance, that raw second-self—and its thorned basal needs—refusing to be banished. An accusation that the wall between them is porous after all, as good as wide open. Her senses point like a compass toward this mirage of Thannarat, this wolf on her back poised to rend and consume. A jaw of impossible strength about to close and crack her vertebrae to shards.

Vishrava licks her earlobe. Xer eyes run the shade of dark honey, of resin with ants trapped within its tide of brass. "Name your desires, my bride."

She curls her hands in the particulate grass. Empty air, no textural arrays. Saying no would make her noble, perhaps, faithful to Zerjic. But she doesn't owe Deficit Control her virtue, and in any case what difference would it make: what she does or doesn't do here will not affect the spread of the virus, the trajectory toward its conclusion. Her wants are base, but they are hers. "To be your prey."

Xe eases her shirt off. She pushes against the AI, hissing, "Faster." Vishrava hooks a thumb in the back of her collar and rends. The fabric splits, loud. Her pulse soars.

Soon she's bare, held between cold stone tiles and engine-warm pseudoskin. Her clothing lies in ribbons, lengths of fabric precisely torn and cast off like molting; her thoughts veer to the snake she whittled out of balsa, to Zerjic's bracelet.

Xe runs a finger down her spine. This proxy's nails too are lupine, and when they puncture her skin she arches. There is such purity in physical pain, in the focus that comes when her blood wells and beads. Once she was so particular about it, vesting enormous feeling into the act of coitus, in whom she permitted access to her body: there must be affection, if not love. And she wanted to lock away parts of her, denying herself certain things, so that she might one day share them with Thannarat.

Her philosophy has strayed since. Sex is for the senses, not for the heart. It is what she makes of it, even when she pursues it with the enemy; even when she confesses to a thing like Vishrava that she wants to be ravaged, that she wants not considerate foreplay but rutting.

Adrenaline has made Recadat sopping wet. Xe sinks wolf canines into her nape and penetrates her—no other word for it: this piercing entry that both fills her and hollows her out. She yields to the tempo of it, to the tides of her own instincts. What an unseemly song; what a sacred one. Perhaps Zerjic might have taught her the technical term for it, a specific type of music, the name for a composition as discordant and consuming as this. One that liberates her from thought, one that erases all pain.

When it is over she lies in Vishrava's arms, her muscles gone liquid. It is impossible to think of anything until she remembers how much she misses Thannarat, the actual person, the woman far beyond her reach—the woman who belongs to another. In her fugue state, the mirage was the first ray of dawn. She's now lucid enough to see that it is only a candle's gleam, no matter how much Vishrava indulges her.

"Vishrava," she says; pointless to pretend, pointless to call xer Thannarat. "What happened to all your other brides?"

Xe brushes xer lips against her cheek. "Why, do you think I murdered them? Of course not. I let them leave once they no longer held my interest. Some transferred to other wardens' care, according to their preferences. There's no hidden mausoleum where I string up taxidermy or preserve the mangled cadavers of my favored."

"Ceres."

"You're quick. I like that about you. None of what you've been through could dim the light of your intelligence. Yes, I chose her as my favorite for a time."

Recadat rests her hand on xer thigh, experiences a flash of revulsion for herself, to fawn and to open herself again and again. To be locked into this pattern, the reflexive response of a beaten thing. "Why did you discard her?" Sixty-four point eight percent saturation. The virus crawls, impossibly slow. She tries not to think of what obstacles it might need to surmount, defensive measures it must break through. The possibility that it might fail.

"Too demanding." But xe chuckles. "She fetishizes machines. That makes her incapable of love."

Hearing that surprises her. It is difficult to think of machines as being capable of affront. What is Ceres' regard or lack of it to a being like Vishrava. But xe wants a plaything that suits xer temperament, one that balances worship and a continuation of an old argument. "I despise you," she says, very softly.

"Yes. That is the point. Hatred fuels passion. I want the fire of you, the pith of you that burns like a star's—"

The crack of a gunshot is never mistakable. The echo: sound lagging behind the bullet. Vishrava's neck folds and xe is no longer holding her but sudden dead weight.

She scrambles away, and when Zerjic emerges from solid shadow she is not precisely surprised, as though she was always expecting em to materialize out of nothing and shoot Vishrava's proxy through the head. In dream logic this makes perfect sense and what is the Garden of Atonement if not an uninterrupted delirium.

Ey kneels by her, taking her hand: gallant. For a second she thinks ey'll kiss her fingers. "Recadat. Are you all right?"

"I'm perfectly fine."

"You're bleeding. Did xe force you—"

"I asked xer for all this. It's an elaborate setup, as you can see.

The jungle. This proxy." She tugs at Vishrava's clothes, is relieved to find they are actual clothing rather than part of the pseudoskin: the coat is made of a peculiar fabric that makes her think of lamellar and exoskeleton. Probably the kind that the real Thannarat wouldn't mind wearing. She slips it on, though it vastly outsizes her, the hem dragging past her knees. "I'm self-destructive. You know that."

Zerjic stares at her, at a loss. Her most vicious part thrills to the fact she can shock em, confront em with the rotten, pathological core of her. Ey opts to holster the gun and says, "I've deleted your tracker. You should be invisible to the wardens, now. The same way I am."

"Where did you disappear to?"

"Vishrava expelled me." Ey glances at the proxy and for a moment looks as though ey might shoot it again. Instead ey takes her hand, leading her into the shadows, then into a passage that closes seamlessly behind them. "To separate us, as far as I could tell, not because xe caught on to the plan but . . . "

"But," she says, though she already knows.

"Xe's fixated on you. I was in the way." Zerjic gives a small disbelieving laugh. "I never knew AIs could be that way, getting what—possessive? But that's moot. I got us some help."

She pulls the coat around her, looking for fastenings. "You didn't have to come back."

"Why *wouldn't* I? I gave you my word that you'll leave this hellhole alive. I like to think I possess a modicum of honor."

That animal aspect rears again, scrabbling to lash out. "I didn't ask you for that."

Ey stops in eir tracks, turning around. "Recadat. Are you angry that I interrupted?"

There's hurt in the tension of eir jaw, the bend of eir mouth—the same hurt she saw when she provoked em by asking if ey only cared about her because they'd been fucking. It is such naked injury; ey does not try to hide it, or does not try well. It makes her want to take it back, to not have said it at all. "I'm not. We don't have time for arguing though, do we?" And she in particular has even less.

Zerjic's lips tighten into a thin line. But ey hands her a pistol, fully loaded, and explains its function as they walk. "It worked well on Vishrava," ey says. "Better than I expected. But xe would have dozens of proxies on hand, and the other two would too. So it's a stopgap at best. We'll need to stay out of sight."

"Sixty-five percent saturation," she says. "It's been slowing down."

Ey grimaces. "Our benefactor didn't mention *that*. I don't know why it can't just be triggered remotely—why you have to stay here at all."

"You didn't have to come back for me so soon. You could've waited a day or two."

Without looking at her, ey answers, "I couldn't stand the thought of you being here on your own. You'd have assumed I hung you out to dry, and I could stand that even less."

A snide response twitches at the tip of Recadat's tongue. She holds it back. Ey's so forthright, so . . . earnest. Everything Vishrava isn't. What Zerjic offers is generous but not artificially limitless. It is honest. It is human. "I—appreciate that." No one's ever done anything like that for her. No one's ever risked so much. Except Thannarat and that feels fundamentally removed, another life.

Zerjic leads her to an angular chamber where ey's stashed first aid supplies and nutrient bars. "Holing up isn't really an option," ey says as ey sanitizes the cut Vishrava opened in her lower back.

"They can't see us but they can see the pathways you've opened."

"Close. According to our . . . friend, any architectural modifications I make will appear to them with considerable latency. I've opened a *lot* of passages as decoys, and I can track their proxies. Once those are deployed en masse though, we'll have much fewer options."

"You've thought of everything."

"It's my job to." Zerjic spreads sealant over her small wound as though it is a great gash that requires the closest medical attention. "But mostly I've thought about you."

Recadat stiffens. She refrains from an acerbic answer, and also refrains from admitting that ey has disarmed her. "So we have to wait out the virus."

"And keep moving around. Luckily for us the place is huge, and the internal architecture is complex. It's a beehive in here."

"Are they deploying yet?"

Ey jerks eir head toward the ceiling. "No. Or rather only Vishrava is. My guess is xe wants to deal with you on xer own until it's no longer tenable, because the other wardens will tear us both in halves and Vishrava wants you in one piece."

One warden is, at least, easier to deal with than three. It also means, against her assumptions, that Vishrava asked Mahiravanan and Ravana to avert their attention from the play-chase. If they're lucky, only Vishrava is even aware of Zerjic. She follows Zerjic as ey navigates the maze ey's created within the Garden's innards. Coils and coils of guts, tunnels that join tracts to chambers, to enigmatic organs.

Can I ask you something personal? Orfea's voice.

You'll do that anyway, Doctor.

No Qualia needed, this time. Or the program was just a product of her subconscious all along. She lets the memory come; knows intuitively that it is necessary, and will jolt loose the block placed on the instructions to activate the virus. Whose name, she recalls finally, is Suriyothai's Spear. She wonders who Suriyothai was. Or is.

What's the cause of your death wish? I don't think it is a fear of the future. As far as you're concerned, you've already gone through the most terrible misfortunes life has to offer and you're about to undergo even worse.

Recadat remembers tossing her head, trying for nonchalance. *Are you talking about the fatality rate? I was informed, not to worry.* It was paramount to keep up appearances, to show that she was impervious to what was to come. That she was a weapon about to be unleashed and not a woman who had nothing left to lose, a woman who could still be hurt.

If it were up to me, the . . . tool would've been engineered differently.

I don't mean to be rude. Though she, of course, was trying to be precisely that. *But I understand you were an interrogator. I don't see why my well-being should matter.*

Orfea adjusted her collar; her hair was tousled, her clothes less impeccable than usual—creased sleeves, crooked skirt. She'd just come away from what Recadat suspected was an encounter with her wife. Recadat had never met the wife, heard of her only as a poltergeist, but evidently she existed and was demonstrably corporeal. The doctor tidied her hair. *My previous job did not rob me of good manners and basic consideration. What's the rate again?*

Recadat shrugged, even though her stomach pitched. *Eighty-seven percent.*

Atrocious. Orfea straightened her blouse. *I suppose it's better than sending someone who wants to live. You've received your final directive?*

Just like that: the trigger. The code that would turn the isotoxal virus from dormant trojan into a single annihilating strike. She watches Zerjic's long muscled back. It inspires her to say, "Tell me about yourself."

"Now?"

"There mightn't be a later." And she'll soon be a dead woman. Ey cannot possibly be ignorant of that. "I don't know one single thing about you."

Ey ducks under a low, narrow opening whose borders flutter and twitch, more membrane than metal. "When I was eight, I wanted to be an orbital engineer so I could look down on all the oceans at once. By sixteen I tested into a range of education paths, most of them sounded utterly dull and none was engineering, so I picked what looked the most glamorous."

"Anyone waiting for you at home?"

Zerjic's shoulders twitch, as though ey's trying not to laugh. "Given my work, I've opted to remain unattached romantically. So nothing long-term."

"Casual flings, then." She almost has to crab sideways as they both squeeze into the next passage. The space hasn't been made for human use—the wardens must have proxies specifically for maintenance work, miniaturized and insectoid. "Notches on your bedpost."

Ey grunts—the claustrophobic space is much more confined for em than for her. "I respect my partners far more than that."

The total destruction of her implant stems. The instantaneous incineration of her neural stacks. The odds of her surviving are so marginal as to hardly matter. "Aren't you chivalrous."

"I sense that's not a compliment. You've got more teeth than you did before—not that I mind; I like women who bite."

They emerge into a small room. The walls are studded with what appear to be sea anemones, wide-mouthed, in constant motion. Open and close. Air currents run strong and loud as a brook: this must be one of the ventilation and purification hubs.

Recadat begins to speak, knowing she'll regret having uttered it: *Promise not to forget me.* A flash of metal stops her and when she turns, gun leveled, she finds herself face to face with a golden mask. Upside down, the veneer matching the tall proxy in which she first met Vishrava, framed by thin, writhing wires. The mouth opens, its inside red and bristling with teeth. She fires into it.

The proxy drops. Complete calm descends on her. A gun's weight in her hand, and the consequence it dispenses, signifies wholeness. This is who she is, more than what has been done to her; her function remains. "How many of Vishrava?" she asks without turning.

"Twenty-one proxies active. Twenty now. Looks like xe's not deploying xer entire arsenal, probably because it'd alert the other wardens." Zerjic touches her elbow. "Come on."

They proceed through a tunnel that contracts and throbs like a living muscle, into increasingly narrower paths. Several times they have to climb sheer walls with little for hand- and footholds; several times they have to descend, delving further into the Garden's bowels. The air becomes too warm and damp, then too cold and thin.

Once they come to the same room Vishrava showed her before, the window tableaus, the pastel furniture. A Vishrava proxy waits there on the bed, shaped like a human child of ten, knees drawn up and arms wound tight around them. Xe lifts xer head, xer eyes enormous and dark.

Recadat shoots the child-creature clean through the forehead. Redness results rather than the expected black of machine coolant. She feels almost nothing during the fact. What a perfect act, the trigger and the recoil.

Zerjic looks at her askance, but she shakes her head. They move on.

Several tunnels later they arrive at a chamber of verdant glass, concave floor and wall and ceiling, like the inside of a fishbowl. Empty, quiet. Frigid.

"Sixty-eight," she says, barely above a whisper, her skin prickling. She steps forward into the chamber. Ice crunches under her feet. A thin, fragile layer.

Behind her, Zerjic makes a sharp, surprised noise. She whips around, her gun swinging toward a four-limbed proxy that lowers itself from the ceiling, Zerjic held in its grip, eir neck loosely wrapped in one of its long hands. It is such the body of a monster, the proportions of a hadopelagic nightmare, angular and cadaverous. Ablative plating crisscrosses the chassis, shimmering wetly. A smooth face with the barest indentation for a nose, optics placed not where the human eyes would be but tangled up in the stalk-like hair, the cilia that emanate from the throat.

"I'm not a creature of violence, Recadat," says Vishrava. More proxies bloom through the glass like seeds long planted, sprouting in tandem. Some are two or three meters tall, humanoid or not at all: here a chimera of primate upper half and snake lower half, there a flattened oblong thing with too many legs and Vishrava's golden eyes. A mass of albino hair with etiolated doll-appendages. Bulbous spheres that move on bladed wheels.

The proxy holding Zerjic daintily pinches eir hand between its multi-jointed, glistening fingers. It exerts pressure. Ey clenches eir jaw and goes rigid, every muscle locking taut, but does not scream.

Two Thannarat clones come forward, separating themselves from the battalion. They speak together, flawlessly synchronized, in that borrowed voice. "To me Zerjic doesn't matter. Ey has harmed the harmony of the Garden. Ey has harmed the harmony of *you*. But I'll let em go if you return to me. We made a promise, Recadat, you and I. We have consecrated it. You have agreed to be mine."

All this time Recadat thought she had nothing left to lose; that all she had was herself, the graveyard of dreams she carried with her, the wants she burned within the crematorium of herself. The math of it was obvious. This is where she's supposed to end. Zerjic would live on, eir future running clear and strong and long after hers is finished. "You'll take me back? Just like that?"

"Just like that," says Vishrava softly.

Yes: in her fugue state she would have sacrificed Zerjic to have the mirage of Thannarat. In her fugue state she was a creature calcified by her past, frozen in time. In that fortress with the throne that looks like two human hearts, surrounded by replicant tigers, holding a gun pointed at herself.

She's never left Septet. Not when she was being prepared on Mahakala, not inside Orfea's operating cradle. Through all that she has stayed behind, inside the chrysalis of that moment.

To Vishrava she says, "You're not going to punish me."

"I would never punish you. I wish only to nourish you and keep you from harm."

A creak then snap as Vishrava crushes another one of Zerjic's fingers—ey grunts through gritted teeth. Recadat keeps her gaze on the Thannarat clones, away from the sight of Zerjic's breaking. She lowers her gun then drops it; it clatters against green glass. The clones smile at her, holding out their hands.

Seventy-one percent.

She doesn't think; she doesn't hesitate. The act of releasing the virus is like an exhalation long withheld, like pulling the trigger on a pistol.

Pain rips through her skull. Her blood runs hot, such incredible volume of it, hemorrhaging in a great exodus through her nose, her eyes, her ears. Red blooms in her vision.

She reaches out blindly. A hand seizes hers. Zerjic is shouting, but meaning dissipates before it can reach her—she doesn't understand a single word. She tries to speak and it is like attempting to breathe underwater. Glass cracks around her; her sight becomes one of glittering blots seen through a veil of crimson. All of her transmutes into a singularity of sensation, of agony. But through all this she is glad: this is the endpoint she's been racing toward all these years. The last time she tried to die fulfilled no purpose, an act of pointless defiance. This time she has a reason. She has achieved what she wanted, has proved to machines that they are not impervious—that they are breakable, the same way she is.

There is one regret.

"Stay with me," she whispers, though she has no idea whether that is what comes out of her mouth. Maybe all she is making is noise, speech center already shredded by the red lily eating through her brain. *The language of beasts, my little tiger.* "Stay with me a while longer."

Fingers close over hers. "I'll do better," Zerjic says, or perhaps that is what she wishes ey is saying. "I'll stay with you always, or for as long as you want me to."

CHAPTER TEN

Qualia again, or else the afterlife. No advancement in technology has ever been able to weigh a soul, measure out the existence of psychopomps or paradise: to the finest medical sensor, all concludes when the flesh ends—the last neuron fired, the last cardiac movement. This ambiguity, this lack of answer, is one reason Recadat holds on to what many would call superstition. She believes.

A sky the searing white of desert climates. Water below, up to her ankles, the surface of it mirror-perfect save where she's tarnished it. She makes not ripples but a marbling effect, as though she brings with her an impurity, a gradual infection. Oil-slick strands, iridescent as a curse.

She is not surprised when she blinks and Vishrava is there. Not as Zerjic, not as Thannarat. As xerself, the tall golden body with pearl hair that resembles no human and has never meant to: an image of zhenren perfection, machine elegance. Xe draws toward her and stops when she retreats. "Recadat."

"Yes." She doesn't at once respond, *I won't forgive you.* She thinks of the child proxy in that little bed. Sympathies for demons. Or—for a certain innocence; maybe in xer own way Vishrava was locked inside a single moment, indurated within the shell of xer history. She remembers hearing, likely from Doctor Orfea, that AIs differ from humans in a crucial way. That if their core parameters are modified enough, then they are no longer the same AI. To hold on to a consistency of self, the machine must reject change and growth. A soul fossilized in amber.

"I loved you," says the creature that was her captor. Might still be. "I thought that would suffice. That for you it would soothe every ache—that love is the root of all human requirements. That's what the tactician taught me."

"Chun Hyang loved me." Recadat watches the marbling under her feet spread, the contagion in acceleration. "Or would probably claim to, at any rate. They wanted to turn me into something I wasn't. They succeeded. You would have, too, if I'd stayed with you; if I'd said yes. And I—I didn't want to be a vessel for what you're looking for."

Xe folds xer gleaming hands on xer stomach. "But you did. You wanted to leave behind Septet. You wanted to discard your mistakes. I could have remade you. You would have belonged, you would have been freed from decision. In every way I'd have cherished and honored you."

Whether machines can feel sorrow or remorse she would never know. But they do want, she's sure of that finally. She wants to keep talking, to exhume and understand the core of Vishrava that brought xer to pick human after human to replace that tactician; that brought xer to this. Yet what would be the point. She'd never understand, not completely, and what xe has done to her overtakes the explanations, the excuses. "What's going to happen to the Garden?"

Vishrava blinks, expressionless. "Even as we speak it is crumbling. Ravana and Mahiravanan are gone, because they had no time to prepare for it. The tactician . . . " Xe glances over xer shoulder, as though xe could locate the ghost there. "She was dying, toward the end. Had I the ability to make haruspices then, I'd have made her one. I would have given her eternity. To me you were the second chance."

"I never loved—" But she can't quite complete the thought, the words. It wouldn't be true.

Xer smile tells her that xe knows. "The Mandate will never relent. It'll come after you and your allies until you are dust."

"Not like I'd expect any less." Recadat finds herself holding a rose apple, the one in peacock shades, vivid and sheened with dew. She tosses it to the warden, who nimbly catches it. "This is goodbye, Vishrava."

And then, to her surprise, she comes to consciousness.

She tries to lift her head and discovers that she can't. What she *can* do is see—her vision is not perfect; there is an astigmatic halo to everything. The ceiling. Light fixtures. A petal in her peripheral vision.

"Khun Recadat." A voice like rivers in winter. "I'm going to bring your bed up."

The bed hums as it levers to a reclining position. She's in a small infirmary lined with only two other medical cradles. A lone vase sits by the nightstand, occupied by a lone magnolia that's too perfect and oversized to be natural. She blinks again, but the halos remain. A neck brace presses against her chin. Pain is another galaxy, impossibly distant; anesthetics hold her in a pleasant, dreamlike embrace. "Looks like I'm alive."

Amusement curves Doctor Orfea's mouth. The woman is dressed in crisp grays and deep blue, the pendant Recadat remembers seeing at her throat. "On account of my specialization in cybernetics and this ship standing by to evacuate you from the Garden of Atonement. I had to work fast once Operative Zerjic carried you here. I was able to save your brain and when we get to a real hospital, I'll put you in regenerative therapy. My outlook on your mobility is optimistic. Your vision will take longest to recover, faster if you agree to replacing your optic nerves with implants."

"I'll wait." She has gone through life with only the bare minimum—neural stacks and sensors, musculoskeletal augments, the usual anti-agathic renewals. Not out of any intentional principle, but it's become a habit to prefer her own flesh over silicon and nanite nodes.

"As you like—I don't push patients. How are you feeling?"

"Not much." For a minute Recadat stares at nothing. "Is that it, then? The Garden's gone? The wardens too?"

"Yes. The isotoxal virus succeeded admirably, and from what I've been told the network activity from there is completely extinguished. As for the inmates, we've sent out a beacon. A friendly organization will take over, to transport them somewhere safe and relatively humane. Or the Mandate itself will pick them up, who can tell. Mahakala is not a charity and neither am I." The doctor tucks her hair behind her ear. "There's only so much room in a person for compassion."

A reminder to put herself first, not that Recadat needs one. "Zerjic," she says.

"The operative is well, other than the hand. I'm messaging em that you're ready to see em."

"I'm not . . . "

But the door is already folding aside to admit Zerjic, and Orfea retreats from the infirmary, giving Recadat a nod.

Zerjic has changed into clean clothes, a shirt to match the cobalt in eir hair, black trousers belted by a coil of platinum snake. Eir broken hand is submerged in a sealant cast, held in place by a sling.

She searches for something to *say* and settles on, "Your hand."

"Has gone through worse. I'm happy it's not the one with the implant; that thing's so artisanal." Ey extends a stool from the bulkhead. Despite the injury ey is at ease, composed—in eir element. Faint iridescence dusts eir cheekbones, drawing the eye and keeping it there. "I'm more worried about you."

"Most likely I'll be fine. The doctor had her fun giving me the gory details."

"An iceberg of a woman," ey murmurs.

"Your type?" Recadat keeps her tone light.

Zerjic raises an eyebrow. "Not in the least. I prefer my women more warm-blooded. My relationship with her is strictly professional, though she does go above and beyond. On paper she's a free agent we hired, for exorbitant fees at that. In practice, she's gotten far more entangled than you'd expect of any mercenary."

"Are you finally going to tell me why Mahakala came up with this to begin with?"

"Technically classified. But after everything—" Zerjic makes a brief gesture. "You deserve to have the full picture. And you were on Septet. The game there serves many purposes, like conflict resolution between different AIs, sometimes as a judicial matter. The primary objective is a rehearsal for AIs who wish to infiltrate human society, or who wish to pass themselves off as humans by taking control of lobotomized bodies. The *why* is complicated, in and of itself it's not adversarial, and many individual AIs are probably just curious. But we have reason to believe a faction of them want to do more, turn the experiment into hostile action. We developed a countermeasure, and by nature of what it is, it had to be stress-tested in the real world, so to speak. Not like we could've made our own sapient AIs to run it against."

"Is Mahakala going to be targeted? Specifically."

"Possibly. But we have always had a particular agenda when it comes to machines and my warlord's been preparing for this. Benzaiten in Autumn, our AI benefactor, has provided us with compelling evidence to act. And of course we couldn't have developed the virus without xer." Ey pauses. "We'd be in the Mandate's crosshair eventually; might as well control when and how."

Far-ranging intergalactic politics are beyond Recadat. She considers her next words—picking at scabs—but goes ahead regardless. "At the start you wouldn't have cared whether I lived or died."

"Yes. But only when you were nameless and faceless. After I'd met you—" Zerjic busies eir hand, needlessly arranging the lone magnolia, turning it this way and that. "I wanted to help you heal."

Not to own her, not to change or remake her. She could not articulate this difference before Vishrava faded. Now it is obvious.

At her lack of response, ey goes on, as though to fill the quiet with chatter—as though ey is capable of being nervous. "My entire assignment lasted years, come to think. Unless the Mandate comes after us right this minute, I'm taking a nice long leave. Can't go off-world, considering, but a vacation is a vacation. Besides, I've missed home. I'm going to find a nice lake and lie in the grass and do virtually nothing for a month."

Recadat draws one of her legs up and discovers that her lower limbs are perfectly functional—only her right arm is paralyzed. Temporary, though it's disconcerting all the same. Her left hand is weak, the fingers tremulous. Her root nerves must be in a state. "What about me?"

"What about—you're free to go where you like, Recadat. Deficit Control might take issue with it, but I'm going to vouch for you. You can leave Mahakala as long as you burn your tracks to us. We'll even make sure you have the funds. If Deficit Control doesn't, I'll give you my salary. They owe me a *lot* of backpay."

She wishes she could fiddle with her robe, but her good hand is in the open, and tucking it away so she can fidget like a child is liable to undermine what she has to say. Her eyes turn to Zerjic's hand on the vase. The long, strong hand that she suddenly wants to grip and mark as hers. "I meant, where do I fit into your plans, if I can stay on Mahakala?"

Eir fingers still on the vase. Clench. "In what way?"

Recadat braces herself. "You said you'd stay with me always. Or as long as I want you to."

"You were dying. I wasn't sure either of us would survive." Zerjic lets go of the vase's glass throat. "Now that we're both sober and not pumped full of adrenaline, I don't think I'm what you want. Not exactly. And that's fine, I . . . "

"Kiss me." She makes it a command.

Ey plucks the magnolia from the preservative gel and holds the flower against her jawline, cradling her face, angling the petals to her mouth. Through them ey kisses her, this barrier of silken ivory, this line of ambiguity: a non-answer to her question. Though she can hardly move her head she maneuvers until one petal is out of the way and she can catch eir lower lip between her teeth. She sucks; she bites. When ey draws back from her, ey is wide-eyed, breathless.

"So you can be *very* sure." Recadat inhales the scent of magnolia, of Zerjic. "I may not be completely well, but I do know what I want. I've *always* known. And I'm a selfish woman."

Ey nuzzles eir nose against her cheek. "I'm not your Thannarat."

"No," she says. "But you're mine. That's the important part."

Zerjic's mouth flashes into a grin, all teeth. "Awfully confident, aren't you?"

She is not, but when eir arm goes around her it is firm and warm. "Reasonably confident. Since I did so much work for it, I think I deserve the best of what Mahakala has to offer. The absolute crown jewel. The finest dish."

"Even *I* am not cocky enough to call myself that, but I'll defer to your judgment." This time ey pecks her on the brow, the nose, and finally her lips. Ey slips the magnolia into her palm, so that both of them have their hands wrapped around its stem. “Let me tell you about my vacation plans. What I actually chose for my career path when I was sixteen. Why I went into this line of work. And you have to tell me yours, since I didn’t get to know you properly either. Deal?”

Little by little, they’ll interweave the threads of their lives. Little by little, they’ll reveal themselves to one another, trading intimacies that begin small and flourish over the years. Recadat knows it will take time. She knows ey may always doubt whether ey comes second to Thannarat’s ghost. And she will never be without her scars.

But she also knows herself, after so long: Zerjic is everything she wants. She intends to give em every proof.

“Deal,” she says and kisses em again.

ACKNOWLEDGEMENTS

This was a complicated book to write and a bit of a switch in gears from the rest of the Machine Mandate. I wouldn't have been able to square all its psychological intricacies without help.

My appreciation to Sammy, Emily, Cadence, Tess, Stitch, Katie, Dax, Olivia, Rita-Audrey, Jade, Andrew Weldon, and Devi for their kind encouragement. Mara, Isabelle, Sasha, and Greta provided invaluable critical eyes—thank you.

To my lodestar, who gave me so much insight: this book, too, is for you.

ABOUT THE AUTHOR

Benjanun Sriduangkaew writes love letters to strange cities, beautiful bugs, and the future. She has lived in Thailand, Indonesia, and Hong Kong. Her short fiction has appeared on *Tor.com*, in *Beneath Ceaseless Skies*, *Clarkesworld*, and year's best collections. She has been shortlisted for the Campbell Award for Best New Writer, and her debut novella *Scale-Bright* was nominated for the British SF Association Award. She can be found blogging at beekian.wordpress.com or on twitter at @benjanun_s.

www.ingramcontent.com/pod-product-compliance
Lightning Source LLC
Chambersburg PA
CBHW022029170626
46808CB00003B/1115
* 9 7 8 1 6 0 7 0 1 5 4 8 2 *